The Unsustainable Systems

Book II of the Welcome & Goodbye, Earth series

Benjamin Wuyts

THE WELCOME & GOODBYE, EARTH UNIVERSE
IN ORDER OF PUBLICATION:

<u>WELCOME & GOODBYE, EARTH</u>
Welcome & Goodbye, Earth: Chapters 1–6
The Unsustainable Systems: Chapters 7–17
The Volgarian Promise: Chapters 18–33
The Masters of Yesteryear: Chapters 34–42

<u>UNDER THE SKIN</u>
Under the Skin: Chapters 1–6
The Unwanted Help: Chapters 7–16

THE WELCOME & GOODBYE, EARTH UNIVERSE
IN CHRONOLOGICAL ORDER:

<u>WELCOME & GOODBYE, EARTH</u>
Welcome & Goodbye, Earth: Chapters 1–6
The Unsustainable Systems: Chapters 7–17
The Volgarian Promise: Chapters 18–33

<u>UNDER THE SKIN</u>
Under the Skin: Chapters 1–6
The Unwanted Help: Chapters 7–16

<u>WELCOME & GOODBYE, EARTH</u>
The Masters of Yesteryear: Chapters 34–42

The Unsustainable Systems is © 2025 by Benjamin Wuyts

This edition published 2026

ISBN: 978-99987-829-3-8

Developmental edit done by Ian O'Reilly
Copy-edit & proofreading done by Gwyn Kipling
Cover design and layout done by Studio Heta

To the knowledge of the author, no artificial intelligence
was used in the final version of this book.

Author's note:

Dear Reader.

I am not perfect. The people that helped me
finish this project are not perfect. This book is not
perfect. Let's be honest, no one really is.

SO…

Should you happen to come across any errors, be they
related to the story, grammar, spelling, punctuation, etc.,
know then that you are always at the liberty of calling me
out on it so that I can correct them at a later stage.

Furthermore.

If you have questions or ideas – it could be
something that you'd like me to include in it – about
'The Welcome & Goodbye, Earth series', whatever those
questions are, then don't hesitate to contact me.

I would like to thank you for purchasing this
book, and helping out the author!

www.benjaminwuyts.com

Dedication:

For Luna,

Who, whilst hoping to score a cookie, on multiple occasions
not only looked over my shoulder while I was typing away
but literally sighed, laughed, and mocked me only to then
tell me not to bother, after which our four-legged pet
decide to try her luck with my wife in the other room.

– Who's laughing now? –

CONTENTS

CAST OF CHARACTERS

Altar; Human, Administrator.

Amarran; Human, Cattarian.

Anaÿa; Djockar, Mortal, Cattarian. (Deceased)

AnonymousPerson329; Anonymous sender.

Arn; Djockar.

Aya; Human, Guardian of Zan.

Babs; Human.

Blex; Anonymous blogger.

Bruut; Treem.

DD2; Ship-Arti, Designated to Aya, Guardian of Zan.

DD8; Ship-Arti, Designated to Fenring, Guardian of Zan.

Dropp; Quaat, Captain of the Quaat ship of war: Boomer.

Ehben; Djockar.

Einar; Spokesperson for the PWPC. (Long since deceased)

Eon; Arti.

Fenring; Thurrock, Guardian of Zan.

Ghala; Medotorian.

Han To; Administrator of the Zanzia system. (Long since deceased)

Hanip; Ship- and Planetary-Arti. Only remaining Arti from the time of the First Ones.

Hot_69_Stuff; Username of a criminal, employed by the Silver Moon.

Inna; Olankan.

Jara; Human, Crime Boss. (Deceased)

Kotar; Human, Mortal, Cattarian.

Loréna; Human.

Moofa; Member of the Guardian High Council.

Niftiti; Medotorian. Partner of Ghala, the Medotorian.

Oni; Crom.

Remus; Human.

Rhynaiia; Djockar. Partner of Ehben, the Djockar.

Rosa; Human. (Deceased)

Sam Jacobs; Human, Mortal, Cattarian.
Soren; K'Tarrian.
T750C; Arti.
Tartan; Member of the Guardian High Council.
Tharo; Human, Cattarian.

FOREWORD

To the Human that is about to embark on the journey that lies
ahead. Wherever you are, in whatever version you are reading
this book, be it on paper, digital, or audio (one day), whether
you have bought it or borrowed it from a friend, thank you
for giving this small-time indie author the chance to show you
the end result of an idea that started somewhere in the Spring
of either 2009 or 2010. I am a slow writer who has made a lot
of mistakes on the way but I can finally say that I'm proud to
self-publish these works in what is currently 2025 / 2026.

As was mentioned in volume 1 of 'Welcome & Goodbye, Earth',
the second instalment of 'The Unsustainable Systems' within the
'Welcome & Goodbye, Earth' series is part of what is currently
a tetralogy that in my mind was originally intended to be one
massive book with a word count that was way too high. I would
like to express my thanks to you, the reader, for giving this indie
author the chance to show you a glimpse into the wellspring that
is his imagination. I hope you enjoy reading this book and that
once finished, you will definitely continue with volumes 3 and 4.

Enjoy the reading and again, thank you.

Benjamin Wuyts

Despite the seemingly endless stars and planets in the vast universe, the mystery of why there has been no contact with intelligent aliens remains unsolved. This fascinating mystery reveals a realm of speculation and adventure, where countless explanations and discoveries are waiting to be unravelled.

PREVIOUSLY ON THE 'WELCOME & GOODBYE, EARTH' SERIES,

Welcome & Goodbye, Earth

Sam Jacobs is about to get his morning coffee from his favourite coffee bar. Next thing he knows, he wakes up from a 352 year-long cryogenic sleep on a spaceship called the Dévara. Its only other occupant is Tharo, a Human of another planet and member of the mysterious Cattarian Order. Instead of drinking his coffee, Sam now has to learn all about mankind and Earth's place amongst the stars and who exactly the Cattarians are. And then, just as Tharo is explaining about their destination, an emergency message from Anonymous-Person329 causes them to divert from their course and mount a rescue mission on the planet of Zanza...

Now for the continuation.

ARCHIVE FOOTAGE OF THE PWPC IN THE ZAN CHRONICLES.

Session organised by the United Worlds of Man
following a review of the Habitability List.
Terra (UTS): 463,012 BC

Moofa: This hearing will no doubt be described in the Zan Chronicles as a historic moment, for which you are present en-masse. It is historic because every member of the Remaining Ten has demanded this session. It will determine the direction in which we will steer the fate of Zan. This meeting is also historic because instead of taking place in our 'usual' Courtrooms, we will, at the request of those who feel neglected, instead hold a public hearing here on what the locals call "the roof of Osthopat" or for those not familiar with it, a pedestal theatre with the metropolis beneath our feet.

You requested the appointment of an impartial judge, which was initially going to be a Volgarian, but since our requests have unfortunately gone unanswered, that role has been transferred to a Guardian of Zan. My name is Moofa and I sit, for those who do not know me, on the Guardian High Command of Zan. I therefore thank both parties who had to agree to this for trusting me. Now, the issue that led to this session aside, we shall answer the following question: should it be possible for the results of popular votes to be nullified if the disadvantaged party believes that the consequences of this decision are too extreme for the future of Zan? If so, that would mean the end of a tradition that was introduced using the decision-making implants since the beginning of our current 55th Age. Deputy Einar, I see on my communicator that you would like to take the floor. As spokesperson for the Planetary Welfare and Preservation Commission, do you wish to add anything?

Einar: The PWPC would like to, Chairman. I would like to take this opportunity by saying that you coming here, this entire show, because that is what this is, should not have been necessary. We could have just as easily organised this session via the galactic net. The PWPC feels this would certainly be better, especially as our decisions can be... sensitive in nature.

Moofa: I don't think the other side will agree to that request. Administrator Han To, of the United Worlds of Man?

Han To: Absolutely right. You will have to excuse the words I am about to use, Deputy Einar, but if that is indeed your way of thinking, if for you a planet is nothing more than a troublesome stain that you can just wipe away, then I suggest that after an undoubtedly excellent record of service, the PWPC should put you in well-deserved retirement. One does not simply discuss the fate of over a million planets in this territory alone through an online medium! You do that with respect for the worlds you wish to nullify on just such a world! The delegation of the PWPC, the representatives of the Guilds, the various Administrators of the Remaining Ten who are currently struggling with the same problem, you too, Chairman and the many residents of Zanza definitely needed to come together here so that everyone, every Zanese person, can see with their own eyes exactly what it would be giving up.

Einar: That Zanza is a paradise for many is something that you could have also shown me online, Administrator Han To, and then I would not have had to spend weeks in LDT to come all the way here! Chairman, the PWPC is in the right on this issue. I do not know what the aggrieved here wish to throw in our direction but it will not change our decision on tightening the criteria that a planet must meet, which is a justified decision and also a correct one. The PWPC has simply done only what the Zanese people have asked us to do.

In fact, almost everyone here, and I have it here on my communicator written in black and white, themselves voted in favour on the question of seeking alternative ways of obtaining resources in Zan. So, when we Zanese accepted the PWPC proposal to raise the living standards across the Habitability List, that plan was overwhelmingly encouraged.

Han To: You know as well as I do that the people did not fully realise how big the implications about such a decision could be.

Moofa: Careful, Administrator Han To. Even the highest ranking among us do not evade the consequences of baseless accusations.

Einar: I couldn't agree more, Chairman. Is the Administrator really insinuating that the PWPC deliberately withheld information? Before the Administrator answers that, it is important to realise that all the rules involved in making such proposals have been perfectly followed and those who propose them can be severely punished if it is found that malicious intent was involved or information was deliberately withheld.

Han To: That no malicious intent was involved I have no doubt. But that does not mean there was no hidden agenda.

Moofa: You are drifting away from the subject at hand. Deputy Einar. You do not have to answer this.

Einar: I have nothing to hide, Chairman. I am just one person in an organisation that employs many millions. To my knowledge, there is no hidden agenda. The PWPC is only concerned with the welfare and preservation of the celestial bodies. It does so with a questionnaire containing a whopping 500 questions. Information that we convert to a scoring system with a maximum of 250 points. All we did, again on the people's demand, was to introduce a tightening of the criteria a planet must meet.

Han To: And does the PWPC then not see what the implications will be if it does indeed execute these decisions?

Einar: The PWPC sees that but is not concerned with it because it has no other choice other than to comply. We do our work independently, that is, without any outside interference, solely on the demand of what the people want. Only with another vote can this be reversed, unless of course our chairman decides otherwise, but then I would add that this is completely against what the decision-making implants were initially introduced for. A Zan containing a democracy of, for, and by the people.

Moofa: My apologies, Deputy, but I would like to quickly correct you on that, just so that everyone understands. The decision-making implants are and have always been playing an important part in our history. They are used solely for voting and election purposes. So just to be clear, it's our way of life. Within this, democracy would in fact be altered if we decide to change the way we decide upon things.

Einar: That is indeed true, Chairman Moofa. The PWPC however does not know what else it can do or say to make that clear. We only respect the wishes of the people and if you decide to nullify that, now or anytime in the future, we will of course respect that decision and reverse our criteria regarding the Habitability List.

Moofa: It is indeed a fact. I want to make this clear to everyone that the will of the people has to be respected. Therefore, no one here blames the PWPC for anything. The PWPC also knows that if they do not do what the people expect of them, there will be very severe legal consequences. In other words, we Guardians of Zan have to then sort it out. These Guardians of Zan are only there for the people. We have no decision-making implants and respect their decisions. We have always done so since the beginning of the 55th Age but how far should we go in that? Is it not also up to us to protect each and every Zanese and their descendants also from themselves? That is what needs to be decided here and, thus, in the other Territories of the Remaining Ten.

Since the start of the 55th Age, the Volgarians did not exactly predict a very good future for us. We are in an Age where, according to them, we will slowly but surely begin to feel the shortage of raw materials. Today, the shortage of building materials is starting to become a serious problem and I fear for what lies ahead. But how extreme are we willing to go to get all of that in the future? What if someone comes up with the idea of not just giving up on planets by no longer maintaining them but throwing entire planets, entire stations, or even worse, living beings into disintegrators? What if the criteria around this start to get increasingly more relaxed, while at the same time being cheered by a general public? When the disintegrators first appeared on the black market, this was already happening in criminal environments and with serious consequences. Is that where we want to go back to but, this time, approved by the people? If so, who will ultimately be responsible for this? On whom should the inhabitants of Zan direct their anger when things start to get out of hand in the future?

Han To: Chairman. If paradise worlds like Zanza have to be abandoned because their preservation has become too costly, it will eventually be the Remaining Ten who will be blamed when they have no option but to withdraw from the area completely. Given that renting a star-attenuator is quite costly, that too will disappear with our departure, and then the frying of Zanza, the disappearance of its water, its jungle and all life, will happen faster and faster. That is what will happen. The planet will die and wither away and with it, I imagine, will come a lot of hatred, violence and endless streams of refugees. Residents with a grudge against the Remaining Ten, seeking a better life on other planets or stations. I will be long gone by then but worry for what will happen as the PWPC becomes ever more stringent to conserve much-needed building materials, and planet after planet withers away until there is nothing left of it....

CHAPTER 7

Zan: 1983, 55th A.o.Z., a.V.E.

Monster-Méridia Calendar: 1.05.024;

Méridia-Archive Calendar: 2.18;

Terra (UTS): 2628.08.14

Dévara, Zanzia System, Sattar Province, The United
Worlds of Man, Gamma A, Third Circle, Zan

Aboard the Dévara, the days soon became weeks. Sam saw his first full month after waking up pass him by. Many months made a year and so the following years kept coming. It took a total of 232 years before the Dévara would come out of the LDT again. After more than half a millennium since Anaÿa took him from Terra, Sam would finally feel a planet under his feet again. A planet whose name Tharo very deliberately kept to himself so that Sam would focus on nothing but his training.

From the helm, Sam had a grandiose view. The window above the control panel offered him the spectacle of the long-distance tunnel: neutrino sparks, uncharged particles smaller than an atom that shot through the cosmos at several times the speed of light, that were stopped by the shield around the ship.

After Tharo had deactivated the LDT-engines just before entering the system, as per protocol, the spectacle stopped and the ship proceeded much more slowly, only at light speed. Sam saw a dot approaching in the darkness. Zanzia, a star surrounded by its fourteen planets. The second inner planet, an orange sphere, was their destination. In mere minutes, they passed four of its moons. In the light of the nearby star, the planet cast an orange glow on the observation window in the helm. She looked beautiful, with her rapidly approaching mountain ranges, canyons and cloud patches.

Something in Sam's heart twitched. He might not know much about the Zan galaxy yet but there were some things that were a constant. There had to be a dark side to such beauty, right?

"Zanza," Tharo pointed out. "Under the scorching heat of her star, this planet would have fried long ago, were it not for the fact that the United Worlds of Man have always reinforced her atmospheric layers in the past. Until the people eventually had enough. Maintaining a planet takes a lot of resources, and they themselves had to provide the raw materials too. In other words, they had given up, pulled the plug on it for good, resulting in its neglect and the necessary tensions among untold generations who did not take the free offer to move to another planet or station when they had the chance at the time. The last time I was here, all that was still pretty green. That was long before there was even a resource crisis. I never expected it to turn out like this."

Sam seemed quite impressed. "This gives me huge Dune or Tatooine vibes."

Tharo looked at him as if he had just grown a new head. "Dune or Tatooine?"

"You know, my penchant for science fiction and fantasy settings?"

"Aah." Comprehension dawned on Tharo's face. "Your planet's mythological speculation. Yes, I recall. I have been delving into that obsession of yours."

"Star..." Sam began.

"Trek!" interrupted Tharo, knowing that it would rile Sam up somewhat.

Suddenly, a voice boomed over the control panel. "Crew of the Dévara! Our scanners have detected your vessel coming out of the LDT and have successfully received the required ID-code. Please turn your ship to these landing coordinates and, once inside the spaceport, register your ship with the harbour master." On the screen, the coordinates appeared.

Tharo pressed a button. "Dévara to Zanza ground control. We

have received the coordinates and are initiating landing. Contact with the atmosphere in five seconds." He released the button.

"An ID-code," began Sam, who had seen the term pass in his studies, "That, if I'm correct, is some kind of ship's registration number, isn't it?"

Through the helm window, patches of yellow, orange and red plasma began to burn. The Dévara had entered Zanza's atmosphere.

"More or less. It is a form of identification that you can send out to all those present in a planetary system, and on stations and ships if you have just left the LDT. With the signal you send out, you give them information about yourself. The longer your criminal record, the more likely you are not allowed to land."

"Can send out? So, it's not even mandatory? Isn't that illogical?"

The flames became so intense and high that the windows of the control cabin began to polarise.

"I understand your question. The signal is similar to knocking on the door before entering. It is basic courtesy to make your presence and good intentions clear, even if you have a criminal record. Those who fail to do so risk making themselves suspicious and being boarded for inspection." Sam already felt a 'but' coming.

"But this is space, an immeasurable vacuum in which danger can come at you from all sides. Sometimes it is better not to make yourself known when pirates and other organisations can take advantage of that."

The window of the control cabin silently cleared and the men gazed at the planet ahead. The landscape looked pretty barren. From afar, all that orange had looked beautiful but down here, it indicated death and destruction.

Sam had imagined his first alien world quite differently. Fortunately, he had already been introduced to more picturesque planets in the bond, among others.

He saw movement on the horizon. The first signs of a civilisation. He could only make out what it was after they flew over a vast mountain range and the swarming appeared. A spaceport, with ships arriving and leaving the planet, trailing down or up through the skies on long tails of booster rockets. As they got closer, Sam saw more. The spaceport was bustling. Countless ships, some more colossal than others, were parked chaotically. No need to reserve it seemed. If the Dévara found any open space in which she fitted, that was her spot.

Tharo followed his gaze. "Don't be fooled by the number of ships." He had brought the ship above a clearing and started to ground it.

"A lot of these ships are standing idle because the owner has over-stayed and could not pay the parking fine. If a vessel is still here after the legal 5 Méridian thirds, it is requisitioned and an owner who cannot raise the amount during that period is stuck here for an indefinite period. Eventually, if at all, they can hitch-hike with someone else when no one else is available for a pick-up."

"Isn't that a bit extreme?" Sam grimaced.

Tharo shrugged. "That's just how things are on Digital Bell or mineral-poor worlds like Zanza that are no longer controlled by the law enforcers of the territory they are in. This planet here is, to coin a phrase they sometimes use on Terra, akin to the Wild West. So, keep your eyes open but know when to look away because this is not what you would call a welcoming environment. Don't forget that our first and only priority is the secrecy of the cattaran."

Once they had landed, Sam found himself standing before their gun-metal grey loading doors as they started to hiss and part, rolling to the side.

Fierce, bright sunlight met his eyes at once and Sam blinked, although the medical adjustments that pulsed through his blood soon worked their magic and tinted his irises. The loading ramp of the Dévara started moving and a waft of dust and hot air penetrated Sam's lungs. The reality of a possible life on his Dune or Tatooine took him completely off guard. Here in the shade, it was scorching. In the full sun, it had to be at least double whatever heat there was now. If Tharo had not given him a heat-resistant robe, Sam would have been cooked by now.

But he was happy to have his senses diverted. He had looked forward to his first alien planet for years. Now that the time had come to leave the Dévara, his safe home, he was extremely nervous, especially after what Tharo had said about it.

Am I trained enough for this?

What if I forget everything Tharo has taught me?

Does anything that happens in the bond actually count as experience?

"Relax. It will be fine," he said in an attempt to reassure him. What Sam did not know in that moment and what Tharo did not tell him was that the man had everything under control. Literally. Because in even those moments when he seemed completely distracted, he was still in complete control. There was nothing he couldn't see. He had no intention of using the cattaran but was so in control of the situation that he surrounded Sam with a shield without realising it himself.

"Breathe in and out calmly and trust in your own ability but at the same time, don't do anything stupid."

Three metres below the ship, the loading ramp finally hit the ground. It was dead silent. The dust clouds blew here and there between and under the ships as if scavenging for things. Gone was the impression of bustle.

Sam made another attempt to breathe in the warm air. It proved to be no problem. Gravity was a fraction lighter than that on the Dévara and Terra but not enough to bother him.

"Let's go." Tharo stepped off the stage first, closely followed by Sam. He was the first Terran to set foot here, not just on this planet but on any alien planet beyond that of his system. He wished that he could have done more to celebrate this moment but Tharo was moving quickly.

The route to the harbour master was the only exit.

Inside the black robe that reached to his ankles, Sam was quite cool and he had access to some water. Tharo walked as if the heat did not bother him at all.

Further on, somewhere among the ships that varied greatly in shape, Sam heard melodramatic music. The sounds were a bit like a harmonica and came from under a ship half buried in sand. He hoped that he and Tharo would not be stuck here. It was four Elyseves on crates making the music, who had fled the heat under a wing of the ship. On the hull of the ship were five huge slabs of flesh sizzling. One by one, they were turned over by a fifth Elyseve, who had probably drawn the shortest straw.

"Don't mind their stares," said Tharo, who saw that Sam himself was staring at the four long snouts of the white skinned creatures. With their huge, dark eyes, they closely watched their every move.

"Some planets, like here on the surface of Zanza, are no longer habitable for many of the intelligent species. So, you could say that everyone you see walking around here is therefore pretty tough skinned. Physically as well as mentally. If you do see Humans, well, there are those who are stranded here or worse, scum who are no longer welcome within even the coolest places of Zanza, where it is liveable for creatures like Humans."

"So, there are some after all?" Sam tried not to stare back at the two-legged creatures regarding them. Were they dangerous? Were they intelligent? He wondered even as Tharo continued to talk.

"There are subterranean metropolises where its cooler, far away from the surface. But all that said, don't be surprised if the residents here can come off as rude or even hostile. They will do so not because of who you are but what you are. Because of the problems here on Zanza, even the Humans who have lived there for many generations point their fingers at the United Worlds of Man who have given up on all this and left Zanza to the local police forces."

"Can they still leave for better places if they want to?"

Tharo shook his head. "Most of them no longer have the means to do that. The reality today is that overcrowding in Zan means that even the few billion lives on and in Zanza will be forever forgotten. A phenomenon that is happening everywhere these days."

"Due to a lack of minerals?" Sam asked.

Tharo nodded. "Indeed. Hard choices have to be made now. What is still worth saving and what is not?"

"I think I'm beginning to understand why you believe that the war for resources is slowly but surely approaching."

They approached a gate, guarded by a single Arti and three LPF officers. The Local Police Forces typically were a mix of Zanese people but these were beings with the same long, white snouts and black eyes as Sam had seen earlier, wearing bulky black uniforms that looked anything but heat-resistant. Sam could already see them approaching from the shadows.

The Arti, shaped like a human, also served as the harbour master. As they stepped forward, a light flickered in their wrist as they started screening them.

One of the officers approached. "What was your last location before your trip to Zanza?"

"One of the Colonial stations in the Neutral Zone, on the border of Free Space," lied Tharo, who smiled kindly at first.

"What is the reason for your stay here on Zanza?" While the Arti spoke in a voice that was human-approximate, there was something about the phrasing and timing that was off. Even in this most advanced age, Sam remembered, Artis refused to look or sound like biological life and had fought hard and long to create their own identity and more importantly, recognition.

"We are here to resupply," Tharo said evenly.

The officer looked him sternly in the eyes. "The Dévara is your ship?"

Tharo nodded affirmatively as the harbour master checked all this.

"No weapons detected." It sounded vaguely metallic. "Flight details checked and confirmed. Departure from the surface within 96 hours, U.T.S."

"All right," nodded the creature beside the Arti now as it spoke. "Keep your eyes open. Zanza is worse than ever at the moment. Despite the security of our colleagues, more and more innocent travellers and colleagues are being snatched by whoever can profit from them. In addition, we also find ourselves with groups trying to enter the Underground at any cost in search of a better life or in an attempt to destroy that better life."

Sam couldn't resist asking him the question. "And they're not allowed to do that? Seek a better life, I mean."

"By order of the Administrator," the Arti interrupted.

"Not that we have to worry about that I guess but you know what they say, forewarned is forearmed."

The gate slowly pushed aside.

"Welcome to Zanza."

THE DANGERS OF ONLINE DATING IN THE COSMOS, PART 2

Newly published article intended for Page Anonymous

I've never really been strong at puzzles or riddles. This one, however, seems relevant to the situation we find ourselves in though.

There is no war that can break me, for it is in the elusive Méridia that I take shelter.

Planets and civilisations, I have survived them all.

I will always be and know of everything and everyone.

I belong to everyone and stay at all times by their side.

Light does not keep up with me, in LDT-speed I cannot be apprehended.

Yet you can find me, for I am everywhere.

What am I?

I remember a time before technological innovations opened Zan to ordinary citizens. I remember loneliness. I remember the time when a ship in distress could only expect help from itself. Space travel then was anything but fun.

The Thka Decree changed that forever at the time of the Great Equalisation. All sorts of technological innovations were made public and the strangest decoctions, crossovers, and sometimes a few steps backward, were created. On the other hand, the Porok Decree then again created a technological wall, describing many of the extensively tested innovations that were simply too dangerous for the general populous of Zan and why they had to be put away forever.

The Thka Decree, as but one example, brought us the Galactic Net, a web of information that is accessible to all. A medium that, far from the LDT-highways, was distributed through a network of secret satellites exactly one light year apart to the Red Line or bubble surrounding Zan with Méridia in the middle.

So, it is only right that making a blind jump on any ship and in any direction is no longer possible. Social media and the like are everywhere, and if you know how to circumvent the privacy rules a little and know what you are doing in that murky world, finding an individual is considered child's play. Each satellite contains the cosmic address of whoever uses it to visit the Galactic Net. It was therefore particularly easy, when combined with Hot_69_Stuff's registration and DNA verification, to hunt down prey that doesn't move around much.

After a dating app called the Black Hole was taken offline, user Hot_69_Stuff had to turn to other apps to search for their victims. Rosa probably wouldn't have approved but Rosa was dead, and the perpetrators will eventually pay for it with their lives.

At his interrogation by the Guardians who found him first, Hot_69_Stuff already started talking after they cut off the first of his fingers. The man was found to have passed on the information of 262 innocent victims, all women, to an organisation in which he was just a pawn. When I finally emerged to retrieve him from whatever hell the Guardians of Zan had set up for him, he must no doubt have regarded me as his lifesaver. His positivity and his promise to reward me with whatever

I wanted persisted until such a time when I too started doing my thing with him, beginning with the few fingers that remained.

Hot_69_Stuff now consists of 263 chunks. I tried to keep him alive as long as possible with the promise that if he managed to say the answer to my riddle, I would let him go. Which fortunately for us, dear reader, was thus not the case. I tried to get some pleasure out of it but Hot_69_Stuff was weaker than I thought. Who knows how long the others of his organisation will last.

CHAPTER 8

Zan: 1983, 55th A.o.Z., a.V.E.

Monster-Méridia Calendar: 1.05.024;

Méridia-Archive Calendar: 2.18;

Terra (UTS): 2628.08.14

Zanza, Zanzia System, Sattar Province, The United
Worlds of Man, Gamma A, Third Circle, Zan

Crowded and sandy; Sam's first impressions of this low-rise city were not too bad.

Tharo knew this would be an excellent test for the Terran. He knew that Sam had already seen other worlds in the holographic chamber and in the bond but he was curious to see how he would react to the presence of so many different races on a planet where there was a real threat to the Human. What Sam did not know was that Tharo used the cattaran, among other things, to keep a close eye on everything around the Terran himself. Whatever would happen. Tharo would always be able to intervene at the last moment anyway. In the holographic chambers, the fuss had been less intense. There, with the safety mechanism on high, the creatures had consisted only of light.

Although troubled by the heat, Zanza's residents, who throughout the many millennia had come from everywhere within Zan to settle on what once was a paradise world, did not seem to be suffering. Not that they had any direct exposure to the star. Their streets were spanned by wafer-thin, colourful tarpaulins. Some were so full of holes and cracks that they simply let the rays through. The residents habitually walked around the spots of intense light without even noticing them.

Tharo was aware that they were the only 'true' Humans in the crowd. Sam appeared utterly unaware of the hostile looks thrown their way. Yet there was no one to call them on it. Tharo knew this was only due to the Local Police Forces who were continuously (at irregular intervals) patrolling the city.

"That friend of yours we need to get out of here, what does he look like?" Sam asked.

"T750C? He's about this tall." Tharo held his hand about two metres off the ground. "It consists mainly of armoured metal, wiring and electronics."

"An Arti?"

"One I put together myself."

Sam had not seen any Artis in the crowded streets at all, and the only one so far had been the harbour master.

Tharo continued. "But we won't find him here. T750C is not your everyday Arti and they only found that out when they threw him into an arena and left him to his fate. He has already survived nineteen battles and will soon start his twentieth."

Sam looked around. "Arti fights?"

Tharo shook his head. "Not here. In the subterranean metropolises beneath our feet that they have closed off to everything and everyone. Going in there won't be easy. I lost communication with him when the agents overran him which, by the way, cannot have been an easy thing to do. Since then, I suspect they have blocked his communication ability."

They stopped in front of a building. Above the entrance hung a sign that reminded Sam of the exclamation mark at the tourist information offices on Terra.

Sam wanted to step inside but Tharo stopped him. "Wait outside and keep quiet. If anyone asks, say you're an ex-member of a STAL-Zan organisation. The STAL-Zanese abhor technology and the questioner will probably stop then and maybe even show you their sympathy or support."

He did not mention that Sam could be in danger if they found out he was a Terran. Terra may have been incorporated into the Zan society but according to the Azrael Decree, it was in a transitional phase and thus a quarantine meant it was still a forbidden system like the rest of Solaris.

Sam looked around. He was unaware of how dangerous it was for him here. Despite the dark, all-covering poncho, he slowly began to feel the heat.

He was silently growing impatient. Was this now his first real visit to an alien planet? He had imagined it to be more fascinating than just waiting outside while Tharo took care of business in search of a way into one of the subterranean habitats.

He walked further on through the narrow streets, packed with different races. Sam saw people selling phials and straw-coloured fruits that he had no name for. There were scaled people yelling and arguing with each other. The strains of oddly electronic music drifted over the hubbub, played by what appeared to be a snorkel being using a lute. A little way on, he saw flashing neon signs of what could only be a bar. Soon he was standing in front of the door that automatically slid open. Behind it, stairs led down, deeper and deeper underground. The cool air on his face beckoned seductively and the murmurs sounded inviting. Sam hesitated but his curiosity took the better of him and he pressed on.

"Human!"

At first, Sam did not realise at first that the raised voices were directed at him. He only realised it when the laughter, ranting and talking stopped and he saw that all the guests were staring at him as if he were the alien. His curiosity gave way to a sense of unease. Sam realised he might have made a grave mistake.

The bartender snapped at him, "You have no business here!" His large, glassy eyes were green with pale green stripes and black and red dots. They were eyes that seemed to see into the innermost depths of Sam's soul.

Should he stay now or climb back up the stairs to the surface? He felt the knot of anxiety in his stomach.

No! This is the first planet I have stepped foot on. I will not run away! He couldn't just leave this place again without a rebuttal.

"This is a bar," he said with more guts than he felt, "So how about an ice-cold beer?"

Everyone continued to stare at him. After an awkward silence, a regular stood up, whose head was a mass of tentacles that reminded Sam of an octopus. The creature stood in front of Sam and stared at him without flinching. Even Sam now felt how hostile the atmosphere was. Others quietly stood up from their seats. Sam considered making a run for it.

Just as he was about to turn towards the door to leave, the bartender knocked twice on the bar. Everyone sat back down and looked at the green-eyed creature who was now nodding at Sam. The regulars seemed reassured and resumed their conversations.

"We don't have beer," said the barman, once Sam had moved closer "and certainly not anything ice cold." With a clack, the creature placed two cups in front of him, no more than two hollowed-out stones containing a cloudy liquid. It held one up and waited for Sam to do the same out of politeness.

"To the risks we decide on and their unexpected outcomes." He drank and Sam, processing what he saw echoed his gesture, hoping the outcome of this risk would not be too negative. Of the drink, he took no more than a sip. It was surprisingly sweet, tingling in the throat and it seemed to have a stronger effect on the barman than on him.

"What is this?"

"Ordaenian Gator," said the creature. "A drink from the Ordaenian System in the Neutral Zone that is difficult for a Djockar to swallow. If you drink too much of it, you experience a euphoric feeling that can sometimes last for weeks. It is a drink that Humans in these parts normally drink only after knowing what it is and what is in it. But you are obviously not from these parts."

"Let's just say it's all new to me here."

The creature respected Sam's vague reply. Perhaps the Human before him came from one of the few self-sufficient, anti-social groups that needed to know nothing about anything and nobody.

"Do you have a name or do you prefer to be named after your race?"

"Just Sam."

The bartender briefly pointed to himself with his thumb and said, "Arn.

Never met a Sam before. A Sa'Am, on the other hand, I have, in a holy book."

"A holy book like a Bible of sorts? Is this Sa'Am important in it?" the Terran asked curiously.

The bartender made a gesture with his fingers that Sam took as a shrug, and started washing the cups. "Quite so. The whole book is about her. A Prophet of sorts. In Djockar speech, the book is called Sa'Am Kal Diran. Loosely translated, Goddess of Resurrection."

The whole bar then went silent again and the Djockar looked at the entrance again.

"Welcome," he said servant-like and respectful.

Sam looked over his shoulder at the company that had entered and immediately realised he had entered the wrong bar. He saw nine officers armed to the teeth, one of whom Sam recognised from earlier at the port. The creature leading them looked disapprovingly at Sam, a physically young Human who was comfortably having a chat in a bar full of not too friendly-looking creatures.

The officer who recognised Sam said. "You looked far too worried to me and now I know why."

"How can this humble Djockar be of service to you fine gentlemen?"

Their superior did not answer and simply approached. As far as Sam could interpret, the Djockar seemed calm himself, although it was hard to tell past their ogre-like scales, tusks, and greenish skin. Sam, on the other hand, felt anything but at ease. He was not in the right place. Something that the bartender, Arn, also seemed to notice. "I think you came here at the wrong moment, Sam."

The creature came to a halt in front of the bartender but pointed at Sam, "This Human is suspected of exchanging information with a group that calls itself the Freedom Fighters of Zanza."

If Sam in that very moment had something to drink then he would most surely have spit it out in surprise.

"*What!?*" Sam blinked. What was going on here? In what kind of weird situation had he gotten himself into? He had never even heard of the Freedom Fighters of Zanza?

Sam got the sudden inkling that he had walked into the middle of something far more complicated and dangerous than it had first seemed. Tharo had tried to warn him that Zanza was full of underground communities, rebels and reprobates.

Arn had to say something, "This Human just arrived here and simply asked for something to quench his thirst." He looked over his shoulder at the others. "That's a lot of weapons for just a single conspirator."

Apparently, Sam's presence was enough to immediately condemn him as a conspirator.

"Oh, those aren't for him," the LPF creature replied, then said the following to the rest of his entourage. "Arrest the Freedom Fighters. They're all coming with us."

Sam saw only one way out: use the cattaran. Tharo may have urged him that it should only be used in an emergency but it looked as though that moment had come much sooner than he had thought.

Fortunately, it did not come to that. The bartender tapped the stone mug on the counter once, twice, and three times. In that moment, Sam didn't know what hit him. The customers jumped up and threw themselves screaming at the nine creatures in uniform who did not get the chance to fire a single shot. Their superior still resisted but fell prey to a tentacle of the octopus-like creature, which had wrapped itself around its neck and entered its mouth as it opened to scream.

The fight was over in seconds. None of the nine officers had survived.

Sam, not knowing how to react, looked at the drink in his cup, remembered the feeling of euphoria Arn was talking about, and chugged the whole lot in one gulp.

Tharo, who had been standing outside the whole time, ready to intervene, chose that moment to walk in casually.

Once inside, unbeknownst to the barman who was in that moment predisposed, one of the stone cups suddenly made two tapping sounds, marking him as 'safe'.

"I told you to wait." Tharo sounded disappointed but was not. He was smirking. He walked through the palette of blood on the ground that showed where the corpses had been dragged away.

"How did you find me?" Sam asked.

"The cattaran is capable of more than you think."

With a bang, the metal door at the bottom of the stairs came down, and Sam was startled.

"You are either two very stupid Humans or very desperate," said the barman Djockar, still trying to figure out where the both tapping sounds had come from suspiciously.

"Neither," Tharo replied calmly. "We just want access to one of the subterraneans."

"The Underground?" The confusion in the bartender's voice was not played.

"There is no access to the Underground. Not for us anyway. With all the problems going on here, the entrances are guarded more strictly than ever. Anyone who tries it is opting for a certain death."

"And yet we need your help." Tharo said. "You are currently the only ones who can."

The Djockar shook his head. "We cannot help you. Try the information centre. They usually do grant access for tourists like you."

"I just came from there and they too are adamant that we can't get in without an invitation." After a pause, he asked, "Are you a religious man, Djockar?"

"We haven't been for a long time," lied the bartender.

"Then you haven't been off this planet in a while or maybe you never have." It was common knowledge that religions within the Djockar race were on the rise again and that was anything but a good sign. The Djockar religion depended on eye colour. Tharo checked the creatures' eyes. Dominant green with black and red. A race with better looking eyes than a Djockar did not exist.

"So, what of it?"

"Djockars with green eyes worship Adinda and are known to fight all sorts of wrongdoings."

"I was not raised religiously," the bartender lied again.

"And in Zan…," Tharo continued. "There is a lot of exactly that at the moment. I suspect you rebels, freedom fighters or, let us not sugar-coat it, terrorists, as they called you even within the information centre, are waiting for the ideal moment to strike and I think we can help each other in this. I am offering you a unique opportunity."

The Djockar thought about it for a moment but realised that Tharo was right. The Freedom Fighters of Zanza no longer had the luxury of waiting, especially after today's raid, which meant they could no longer stay here. "Agreed. Provided you don't interfere with our plans."

"Provided you give us enough time to manage our own affairs," Tharo said immediately.

"Provided your plans do not interfere with ours," parried the creature.

"Agreed."

"What kind of plan?" asked Sam curiously.

"The destruction of the entire Underground," the bartender said without flinching.

"Wait," said Sam, "you are terrorists then?"

Tharo ignored his question. "How do you plan to handle that?"

"That will come later. If you guys are really serious and want access to the Underground, you need our help as much as we need yours. A member of my organisation, together with a few of our colleagues, managed to shoot a transport ship that had just left the Underground, obtaining a digital map of their entire network. At least, we know it's a map, but it's too heavily protected for any of our Artis."

Tharo nodded understandingly and handed the bartender his communicator. A device with which literally anything could be done, from making holographic calls to piloting a small ship like the Dévara. "My Ship-Arti can handle those. Where is that colleague of yours?"

"He has a huge Falaka farm deep within the agricultural area of this world."

After a few seconds of hesitation, the bartender entered the coordinates into Tharo's communicator. "I haven't heard from him since the incident with the transport ship, so they can't find him. The

LPF's have been increasing the pressure in recent years. Our communications are minimal to avoid getting caught and now that they know we may have sensitive information, they are putting a lot of pressure on the locals. Anyone who looks even slightly suspicious is taken away for questioning."

The bartender walked to the middle of the bar and slid open a trapdoor into which one of the bodies and a pool of blood had already disappeared. A ladder appeared out of one of the walls inside the shaft. "This passage will take you a few blocks away. I will arrange for you to be met there by Ghala, a Medotorian, who will take you to Ehben's farm. Just tell him that Arn sent you."

EXTRACT FROM THE ZAN CHRONICLES

Index: Comic.

Title: The Amazing Adventures of Fenring, Guardian of Zan

The two Guardians of Zan, Fenring and Aya, are on board the ghost ship known as the Brink, and accompanying them is the Quaat Captain whose ship of war, the Boomer had discovered it. They are walking through the dark, emergency-lit corridors and rooms, and there are bits of human and non-human viscera and blood everywhere.

Aya: Have you, in any of the lives you have lived so far, ever experienced anything of this nature?

Fenring: Believe me when I tell you that just when you think it can't get any worse, the opposite will one day surely take place. Again, and again, and again. Until, eventually, the most gruesome of things won't bother you anymore. It can always get more obscene, little one. Bloodier and horrendous, with more violence, and thus with less and less mercy for those who commit them. Which is precisely why only we enter the darkness when the courage to do so diminishes in everyone else.

Aya: Don't call me little one, old man.

Fenring: Forgive my poor choice of words, I sometimes regurgitate something when I focus on a matter that excites me. Everything all right there, Captain? You look a tad anxious. Are you hungry?

Dropp: Don't worry about that, Guardian Fenring. Quaats have caused scenes like this themselves countless times in the past, and so, Guardian Aya, continuing with your colleague's answer, I can indeed confirm that it can always be worse.

Fenring: Aah... the Harvest. It has been a long time since Zan and the planets that were subjected to it have experienced such a thing.

Dropp: And will never experience again.

Fenring: Well, I would never say "never" but indeed, let's hope not.

Dropp: Is this, Guardian, what you saw on the earlier ships as well?

Aya: In exactly the same circumstances even. The score already stands at 25 ships, Captain Dropp. I would advise that you pay attention to where you plant your feet but considering the body parts and blood are literally scattered everywhere, I guess that is hard to do. Instead, just try not to step on the flesh as it is technically still evidence.

(A sticking, sickly moist sound as the three figures move through the gory spectacle)

Fenring: We will do our best. Meanwhile, do we know anything about the Brink that you may have overlooked or have already found among the other ships?

Aya: Well, the way in which whoever is behind this has proceeded is always the same for all twenty-five ships as far as we know. All were refugee ships run by volunteers who, to cover costs, did not have an LDT-drive and were equipped with poor Ship-Artis, all of which had poor security to defend themselves and with even poorer maintenance. Perfect targets, in other words.

Fenring: Do-gooders or not, anyone travelling from A to B outside the LDT-highways without an armed escort or the means to defend themselves know the risks involved. And in that aspect, to borrow a Terran saying, it is like mopping the floor with an open faucet.

Aya: Regrettable but not untrue. Both our Ship-Artis are trying to do what they can to get as much information out of the Brink as possible but I fear that, as with the twenty-four others, it won't make much difference. We know that the ghost ships are all unregistered, that they all came out of high speed when a virus paralysed their operating systems and that the ships ran out of power. We have managed to recover the Ship-Artis afterwards but always with a gap in their memory that starts when they receive the virus and ends when we arrive.

Dropp: There is information from just before they were infected?

Aya: Nothing that can help us further, I'm afraid. The Brink is an old ship with few if any sensors in her hull. The staff sent a lot of messages to the ships and received a virus, which they no doubt thought was an ID-code.

Dropp: In other words, we don't have access to the security systems and at the time of the incident, they were recording nothing anyway! We are nowhere!

Aya: I didn't say that.

Fenring: Aya is right. Your Ship-Arti acted correctly when it had the Brink in its hold. It compared the passenger list with the body parts and blood it found, or rather the DNA, after which it compared that with the information on the galactic net. Our ships also did the same and came to the same conclusion. Of the 12,802 registered occupants, 9,933 are missing.

Aya: Which compared to the ships before, where there were also a lot of missing people by the way, is a record number.

Dropp: There could well be several reasons for that. A Quaat alone could easily disembowel someone like that, which is not to say that Quaats have done this!

Fenring: No traces of Quaat DNA have been found as far as we know. But while we're on the subject, a plausible idea just came to mind. In doing so, this old man, Aya, with all his lives, may have solved one of the biggest questions concerning our little predicament.

Aya: Doubtful, but I am all ears.

Dropp: I have heard a lot about the ingenuity and speed with which an experienced Guardian of Zan can sometimes operate, and I am happy to see that in action now. What have you found out, Guardian Fenring?

Fenring: Of the aggressors who came on board here, we found nothing, which suggests that they were either Artis or that those same aggressors were pretty well wrapped up. Only within the Iron Beast can they tell us if it was the former which, once we asked if a mobile Arti was actually involved, they strongly denied it. Therefore, we must rule out Artis. Besides, there is nothing, Captain, to suggest that the missing occupants left the ship because again, no traces of that have been found. So, if like the remaining victims they were indeed shoved inside someone's mouth, where then are the remains?

Quaats can, as you said yourself, chomp someone's arm, head or you name it up just like that but not without leaving traces. What Quaat would do that while his meal still has his clothes and other belongings on him? Your Armours need meat, not shoes. They may have stripped all of that off but your Ship-Arti, as well as ours, have again found nothing to even hint at Quaat involvement. Meanwhile, we already know that the pieces of passengers left behind have not been eaten. Everything, let's just say, fits and no bite marks have been found. The passengers were torn apart with brute force or were cut open as no implant was left behind and they took from the Brink itself whatever they could.

Aya: Conclusion?

Fenring: We cannot find what we miss because what we miss, organic and non-organic, was literally pulled apart. So, I conclude that all of them, whether they were alive or not, were thrown into the disintegrators and thus converted into usable minerals.

Dropp: Isn't that what your colleague had put in her report earlier?

Aya: Already from the first ship even. Have you actually read any of my investigations into the earlier ships, old man?

Fenring: I am Fenring...

Aya: Meaning?

Fenring: ...I do not read reports and start every case on a new page, with a fresh pair of eyes.

Aya: Before you ask, Captain. The Guardians don't normally operate like this. Fenring is, to put it with the best of intentions, different.

Fenring: Different and better but let's not dwell on my idiosyncrasies. The disintegrators have clearly been tinkered with being able to break down organic material as well. That their existence is a fact is no longer a rumour. The Collector ships and all that goes with it will not be too happy about that. But why not just throw everyone into the disintegrators?

Aya: That's what we need to sort out. Why, who and how. However, the dismemberment of our missing passengers was not haphazard but rather selective and, judging from the previous ships, it wasn't against just one race in particular but rather, many.

Dropp: Thanks to our Ship-Artis, we now also know exactly which races were disintegrated.

Aya: Absolutely right. All races originated from the Great Equalisation. Which perhaps indicates that something inside the substances that the Volgarians used to accomplish that, after even thousands of generations, must clearly yield something of value. The number alone of races that experienced the Great Equalisation runs into the millions. But Humans, even though they did not evolve from it, did not escape it either. Then there are the creatures that generally possess many implants and are thus a bonus when it comes to obtaining minerals. The Thurrock and, of course, Quaats because of their Armour.

Fenring: So it doesn't look good for the three of us; a Human, a Quaat, and a Thurrock! We can assume that the list at their disposal is therefore quite long, and that mainly the Zanese that arose from the Great Equalisation possess more minerals or something other than minerals than everyone else because of that. A theory we can easily test.

Aya: By finding one or several Zanese low lives that are the product of that time and tossing them into a disintegrator that we then have to first sabotage to break down organic material?

Dropp: Which, I take it, is not an option? If so, I absolutely must protest against this.

Aya: It probably won't come to that. At least not from us.

Fenring: Captain Dropp, how motivated is the crew of the Boomer to bring all this to a successful conclusion? Would any of them protest if we place this ship with you as her Captain under my supervision and leave the Quaat Empire?

Dropp: The Guardians of Zan are higher in rank and the crew knows that too. It would require quite a bit of paperwork but eventually they would go to wherever it is that you would take them.

Fenring: Here's a tip for you, Aya. If you've been on the job as long as

I have, you must have already built up an extensive and reliable network of informants.

Aya: Noted. Where are we going?

Fenring: To where the rumours about the sabotaged disintegrators first started. I will contact High Command to state that you will come back to Méridia with a detour. Meanwhile, Captain Dropp, we set course for the Lubliën Province, with the final destination of the Between-Station, Isa.

In Memory of our Fallen Heroes:

The creative team behind the highly popular series of comics, 'The Amazing Adventures of… Guardian of Zan' pays tribute to the Guardians whose epic adventures brought them wherever they needed to be among the stars. While some characters are fictional, altered, or kept private for various reasons, their bravery and dedication to the cause remain real.

We remember those who served, those who gave their all, and those who live on in our stories. These comics are only made possible thanks to the immense amount of data that was given to us by the Guardian High Command, which tells us all we need to know about the missions and ultimate sacrifices of our fallen heroes.

In our vast universe, their memories continue to shine as guiding stars. They remind us of the courage it takes to protect our way of life and the enduring spirit of those who never truly fade away.

THE HUNT FOR BLEX

Newly published article intended for Page Anonymous

Dear readers (of which that number is slowly but surely increasing over the years) and Guardians of Zan. According to news already confirmed by various sources, you are diligently seeking my true identity and I cannot help but wonder why.

I talk about historical events and my encounters with certain historical figures as if I have been there myself. This is true. I write in detail about the sometimes-unnecessary sufferings I have brought upon others and their sometimes-inevitable death. Also, true. But whether or not that is the case, whether or not everything is fictional, I leave that to the imagination of you and the reader. Interpret my texts, my words, and my statements as you see fit.

I tell stories in an attempt to entertain myself in what I can only describe as a boring existence. An existence in which I know has never been mentioned in the Zan Chronicles and is not bound by what we know as the concept of "time."

Realise this: I am always and everywhere. My true face and name will be revealed only when I want it myself. Not before.

In other words, try not to stress about it too much because one thing is certain. No matter how much information you have, whatever you think you know or still want to know about me, and no matter how many of you will come after me. You won't find me, which of course, doesn't mean you can't try.

Either way.

The best of luck.

CHAPTER 9

Zan: 1983, 55th A.o.Z., a.V.E.

Monster-Méridia Calendar: 1.05.024;

Méridia-Archive Calendar: 2.18;

Terra (UTS): 2628.08.14

Zanza, Zanzia System, Sattar Province, The United
Worlds of Man, Gamma A, Third Circle, Zan

As they came out of the tunnel, Sam heard a whispering voice. "Humans..." It had to be Ghala. If only he knew what a Medotorian looked like. That one hadn't come up yet during his studies.

"Ghala?" Sam murmured, spinning in the direction of the voice. Behind them, the hatch to the tunnel slid shut again.

"Arn sent us. He said you can guide us to the estate of Ehben, the Djockar?"

"I am, I know, and indeed I could." There was a shuffle in the darkness as the speaker emerged from what can only have been a secret passage, as Sam heard a hiss and a clunk further behind Ghala.

The alien was a small creature only about ninety centimetres tall. He had the stature and physique of a Human toddler of about two years, but was bald with dark blue skin. His mouth was huge and he had two tiny holes where Sam had expected ears and two large, white eyeballs bulged out of both sides of his narrow little head. He stood less than two metres away from them.

One eye was pointed at Tharo and the other at Sam. It stared at them defensively.

Sam, while frowning, concluded, "Let's assume then that you are Ghala."

"Hey, why the fuck are you looking at me like that?" the creature snarled irritably.

Sam, startled and amused at the same time, for some reason had been under the impression that the universal translator did not process swear words until now. Tharo himself never swore and aside from that, during all of the onboard entertainment from the Dévara, he had never noticed swearing before. He wondered what Ghala had said that made the translator translate it like that.

Tharo put his hand on Sam's shoulder to calm him down.

"Let's get one thing straight," Ghala said venomously. "In this godforsaken part of Zan, one look can be cause for murder. Would you like to die, little man?"

To which the younger Human amongst them could only respond with. "Who are you calling little?"

Tharo, faking amusement, clearly saw the creature contemplating on grabbing his side arm. His minuscule fingers were slowly gliding towards the hilt of its tiny weapon and so he calmly said, "That's enough. We have no intention of harming you or your organisation and their plans. On the contrary. His name is Sam, my name is Tharo, and as you have no doubt heard from Arn, we are working together to gain access to one of the Subterraneans where both ourselves and your people have a certain business to attend to."

Ghala's eyes narrowed. "I have been in the resistance for 25 Méridian Thirds. The Administrator of this planet is a Human. A Human like yourselves who lives a nice and relaxing life with a lot of others of his kind in the coolness under our feet, while the rest of us burn! Not a hair on my head would consider confiding in two random humans right now." He pointed to his bald head.

"Well, you're the only one here who's armed," Sam said delicately. "I imagine it wouldn't end well for you if we got caught."

The Medotorian nodded reluctantly. "It wouldn't end well for all three of us."

The small alien winced, looking at Tharo and Sam a little speculatively for a longer time, and then appeared to make his mind up. The shared threat of any impending punishment by the LPFs had appeared to mollify him somewhat.

"I have a glider not far from here. But we will have to be careful. I know what transpired in the bar a moment ago and the long arm of the law is suspicious of everyone and everything. Even more so if they see the three of us hanging out together."

"We understand that." Tharo was nodding, and appeared more used to these sorts of conversations and spaces. Sam was struck by just how old Tharo was again. If what he had told him before stood as true and if the process of rebirth from within the temple of the First Ones had preserved his life almost indefinitely, then surely he had fought in wars and been a resistance fighter, and been both a criminal and a civilian by now. "Very well. Follow me. Once there, let me go in first to prepare it for flying before you board. Wait for my signal. Also, you probably didn't notice but I'm quite small. In other words, watch where you're walking while following me!"

Distance is relative. What is far for a Medotorian is less than two hundred paces for a grown man. The sturdy Medotorian, with his short legs, took almost five times longer. His stature and poor fitness made him an excellent sneaker but would make him a very poor sprinter.

Ghala led them through the busy streets of the city, easily disappearing behind legs or street chairs as Sam and Tharo followed, before they saw him stop at one of the busier shopping streets, inconspicuously trying to catch his breath. Across the crowded street, dozens of gliders were parked. When Ghala had recovered, he crossed over to run between the large, folded wing vehicles. Because he was so small, he almost got knocked over a few times. Then again, his size meant that he made it across unseen.

"How is he going to pilot it?" Sam whispered to Tharo, looking at each of the large vessels.

In reality, each glider was tiny compared to even a scout ship capable of atmospheric entry. They came in all shapes and sizes, some with fixed wings, and others with quad-copter wings, but each having a bulbous passenger and pilot compartment in their heart.

Sam was reminded of insects as he looked at all of the garishly coloured vehicles around him. Suddenly, there was a rattle from the nearest vessel that Ghala had disappeared behind and its four wings descended, locking into place. A moment later and the four thrusters started, stirring the dust and sand around them in swirls that seemed to bother hardly any of the bystanders.

Tharo and Sam interpreted that as Ghala's signal for them to make their move. It was at that moment that the common people in the shopping streets, rather than the heavily armed enforcers of the law who had been watching the pair, started to notice the two Humans in their midst.

"Humans? Here!"

Alarm and mistrust was quickly rippling through the crowd around them as Sam figured that every Human they had seen must belong to the secretive subterranean, elite complex. Humans brought hate.

They ran for Ghala's vehicle and before Sam's curious eyes, his universal translator changed the illegible signs on the side of the vehicle to the word "taxi." The duo got into the glider and took their seats in the back. Both doors of the vehicle slid up.

Sam looked around interestedly. "Is this what you do for a living? Carrying passengers around for some Digital Bell?"

"This is not the time to have a chat," Ghala whispered irritably from his pilots seat, which was specially modified so that he was much higher, along with a custom flight stick. "Or do you want to kill the three of us so soon already? In that case, I advise you to go right ahead. In fact, why don't you wave your arms around and talk a bit louder?"

Sam immediately shut up. He realised he still had a lot to learn about the universe.

Either that or Ghala, as he would sometimes describe certain people, simply put, was being a dick towards all creatures great and small.

Not that Ghala and the others here didn't have good reason to be angry, Sam considered. He remembered what Tharo had taught him about the resource shortages in Zan, and the effect it was having on everything and everyone. It was today that he had truly seen what that was like.

It was the United Worlds of Man, who in turn complied with what direction the Zanese people wanted Zan to be steered in, that stopped supporting Zanza. Therefore, the planet's surface has become uninhabitable without its atmospheric filters. The richer Humans, together with no doubt a bunch of other species fled underground, still controlling everything, while everyone else starves.

Ghala started the manoeuvrable engines, which spewed out a cone-shaped blue glow, and took them safely into the air.

——

The near-silent vehicle began to pick up more speed. Only when they had well and truly left the city behind them did Ghala speak again, gruffly. "Show me the coordinates of Ehben's farm. I haven't been there in a long time."

Tharo retrieved his communicator from under his clothing, which turned on automatically under his touch. He made a few quick finger movements on the screen and reached forward with the communicator so that Ghala could see the screen with his bulging right eye.

"That's quite a stretch." Ghala did not expect an answer.

He pressed some buttons and a glow came over the window. It was a protective shield of pure energy that domed the upper part of the vessel. The faster they braced over the vast land, the greater the air resistance would become. The shield would make the journey a bit more comfortable and much cooler.

At speeds well above three hundred kilometres per hour, the city was reduced to a dot on the horizon within a moment.

Sam looked over Ghala's shoulder and saw that the speedometer on the instrument panel was not yet even halfway. He was impressed. This vehicle could obviously reach hallucinating speeds. Without that shield, those would undoubtedly be fatal to them. He wondered what it would be like if a bug or even a bird that thrived in temperatures like these would fly into the glider's shield and what it would then be like if that same shield wasn't there.

Tharo leaned back comfortably. "Tell me something, Ghala. You mentioned that you have been a member of the rebel movement here for a whopping twenty-five Méridian Thirds. Why did you join at the time? Were you one of those poor souls that had lost his ship because you overstayed your welcome?"

"Ever since the dockworkers seized my ship," the creature admitted. For the first time since they met him, he sounded somewhat friendly. "They realised I was supplying the residents here with weapons and wanted to intercept me. Due to my size, I was able to go into hiding but yes, I had lost my ship."

Sam only followed the conversation with half an ear. He was glued to the window, looking at the barren landscape about half a kilometre below them. The surface of Zanza was worse (if possible) than any of his fantastical speculations. There were entire deserts of sand so scorched and bleached that they were almost bone white and glaring. There were expanses of rocky massifs with tortured, twisted, and cracked pillars of nothing but brown, baked, stone. Sam could never have ever imagined the size of such a place on his own.

"I lost both my ship and my life partner in one day," Ghala admitted, his voice twisting in rage and frustration. "First my ship and then not much later my wife, Niftiti, who could not escape the law enforcers."

Sam shot a horrified look at Tharo. "Was she shot?"

"The law enforcers here are not that extreme, nor is that not their first course of action, anyway. In our flight, she was simply arrested. Captured because they couldn't get me. Such are the risks of the profession, I'm afraid. I worked on a plan to free her but couldn't find the necessary resources. She died because to them, Niftiti was just another mouth to feed, and so it was more profitable to sell her, after which she was thrown into an arena for the amusement of the residents beneath our feet."

Sam did not know what to reply, and Tharo too remained silent.

Such cruelty, Sam thought. He couldn't imagine it.

It was Ghala who broke the silence. "For over eighty Méridian Thirds we were inseparable, unbelievable. She was literally plucked off the street and less than three days of U.T.S. later, she was swallowed in one bite by a Papara, which I witnessed on a live broadcast."

Sam had to think for a moment what a Papara was again but then it came to mind. An eighteen-legged monster with a long maw like an alligator.

"Does that kind of practice happen here regularly? Picking individuals off the street just like that and then throwing them into an arena?"

"In a place like Zanza? Absolutely. Daily even, because most of the time, contestants receive quite a sum if they actually survive it. If a territory decides it no longer cares about a system, planet or station because maintaining it is too expensive, it means that all personnel, all prosperity, all security goes. Everything disappears. The locals are left behind, after which eventually the vultures come, looking for profit. The local law enforcers do what they can but know themselves that many of them are not exactly working by the book, if they have a book at all. The Administrator of this system should normally keep order and report disorder to the Guardians but I suspect they are just as corrupt, otherwise the Guardians would already be here. They have it easy in the Underground but those who live here on the surface know that any day could be their last. Not only do people disappear for profit into the arenas but more and more ideas are bubbling to the surface that some of us are being thrown into the disintegrators after death or, according to what we heard, even alive."

"Disintegrators?" Sam winced. Whatever that was, it didn't sound nice. The only 'disintegrators' he had seen had been on board Tharo's ship, and it was a device to get rid of waste material with the option to extract moisture or useable minerals from it, or simply to convert it into a power charge.

People do that to people!? Sam thought with a shudder. It was the ultimate cruelty, wasn't it? It had that awful ring of cold-faced economics about it, where something (or someone) useless could be transformed into something economically useful... like water or energy.

But what sort of monster would ever do that?

"That's a pretty disturbing accusation you're making there." Tharo said sternly, stroking his beard. "Throwing organic material, alive or dead, into the disintegrators is as forbidden as entering the forbidden systems."

"Well, so that's how they keep us under wraps. And most of us are too scared to do anything about it," Ghala spat.

The landscape below them and in front of them was a cracked, endless, cork-dry plain, shaped by the blistering sun and lack of water.

"That is the reason I have been fighting all these years and doing what I can to make the Zanese people outside Zanza aware of the crisis we are in, and what can happen when a planet is abandoned and the inhabitants on the surface are left to themselves! Starting with the Underground that doesn't care at all about our situation!"

Sam saw Tharo looking at their surroundings with a grim face. He wondered how many times Tharo had seen worlds like this, and what it must be like to see a world go from healthy to sterile, as his mentor continued to talk.

"Ghala, have you been to any of the Underground cities?" Tharo wanted to know. "After all, what goes on here on the surface, the crime and decay of the planet must undoubtedly also happen within the Subterraneans."

Their pilot pulled a face. "If you don't live there, you don't get in. It's as simple as that. We tried and succeeded one time even before but security has only increased since then."

"Suppose you guys manage to do it all over again then," began Tharo, who did not appear to hold much hope in the Medotorian's plans. "Suppose you guys manage to destroy the Subterranean cities and thereby successfully convey a clear message to the rest of Zan. What then? You will be branded as an extreme terrorist organisation and hunted down to the last man, and in the very worst case, that might extend to everyone on the surface. What kind of impact do you think you can make on the United Worlds of Man and on Zan when this kind of situation, in some cases much more extreme even than here, is happening everywhere? Do you not see that Zan itself is dying?"

"I am a fighter, not a thinker. What I know is that each of us is willing to give our lives for the cause. That's how dedicated we are.

Our goal is to give the four billion-plus inhabitants living under our feet as kings a message that they will never forget in Zan. In so doing so, hopefully the rest of Zan will realise that you cannot just abandon a planet. Who knows, maybe we will inspire others to do the same."

That sounded a bit overconfident to even Sam's ears. He and Tharo wisely decided not to discuss it further. Tharo didn't really care either what this group wanted to do or not. He needed something that they could provide without making too big of a scene, the getting in part. It was as simple as that. The less he had to use the cattaran, the better. They didn't want their distrustful, temperamental guide to decide to give up.

Tharo looked glum, and Sam wondered whether he had just as pessimistic view of their claims as he did.

A small light started to flicker on the screen. Tharo and Ghala silently watched a hologram be projected on the instrument panel.

"What's wrong?" asked Sam slightly alarmed.

"A sandstorm," Tharo said briefly. He looked worriedly at the horizon.

Sam saw that it had disappeared. In its place had come a dark orange wall. Even from a great distance, he could see that it was sky-high and coming towards them at blazing speed.

"That sand is coming from the Haraka plain," Ghala said darkly. He did not hesitate to fire up the engines until the speedometer was almost at the top.

"Why is that bad news?" Sam asked.

"The Haraka Plain covers a good chunk of the northern hemisphere of this planet. On that side, the surface is subjected to extreme temperatures."

Sam remembered his heat-resistant robe and thought, "And in the city they weren't?"

Tharo saw Sam's confusion and explained: "Storms this dark and this hot point to only one thing. Glass. And on planets like these, the cities are usually protected by shields."

Sam looked at him incredulously. "You mean... that storm is so hot that the sand inside has turned to glass?"

"That's right. I've been in such storms before but with vehicles that were fully covered with a shield.""

"Unfortunately, this cheap model does not have that," said their driver. "And in any a normal situation, each and every glider is supposed to turn back to either their point of origin or divert to just another city. But no need to worry. With any luck, we should be able to outrun the storm."

"Should?" Sam felt a tremor of panic.

"Just trying to give our young travelling companion some encouragement," Ghala laughed. "No, I'm afraid to say that unless we turn back, we'll be right in the middle of it."

Sam grew more anxious by the second at the sight of the dark creature racing towards them.

"But like I said, no need to worry about that. I'm the best pilot there is. And I always keep my cool."

Tough talk, Sam thought.

Tharo, on the other hand, knew that Medotorians remained icily cool in the most stressful of situations. He could imagine that Ghala's wife had also fearlessly met her end.

"Besides, I know this landscape like the back of my hand. We can't fly over the storm because this glider can't handle that. Flying through it is pure suicide. Therefore, the only thing left for us is to do is to fly under it at an oblique angle and hope the storm has passed when we re-surface."

"Resurface? Out of what? Water?" pondered Sam but he said, "Can this thing go underwater then?"

"Don't be stupid," said Ghala. "This model is not designed for that." He tapped on the map. "If we can reach the ruins in time, we could find cover there from the storm." From above, the ruins looked like a child's drawing of the sun, a circle with squiggly lines around it representing the sun's rays.

Behind the ruins, Sam saw another zone begin on the map and it was actually green. The agricultural zone that included Ehben's farm, he supposed. "How long until we arrive?"

"I can only say exactly once we reach the maximum speed of this thin can but approximately, just under half an hour until we reach the gorge. Once in there, we have to slow down at every turn, so it will take over an hour to get out. If the storm doesn't get us first, at least."

It didn't take long for the indicator to reach the maximum one thousand kilometres per hour. Below them, the ground raced past. With no details, Sam couldn't see anything from before. The whole thing began to shake under the tremendous speed. Ghala reassured them that the glider could definitely handle it. He would know, for he had driven it up to such speeds himself.

When they arrived at the gorge, Sam looked back at the approaching storm. The dark orange wall made of the grains of both glass and sand seemed twenty times higher by now, stretching from the desert sands all the way up to tower in the sky. Ghala had not exaggerated when he had said that flying over it was not an option; it looked as though the storm raged as high as the atmosphere.

Sam looked forwards, towards the gorge. When he had been wandering around on Terra, he had visited the Grand Canyon, and he had already struggled to really grasp the magnitude of it. Later, he had read about the planet Mars, which featured the largest canyon in the entire Solaris system, dwarfing the Grand Canyon. The canyon he was looking at now seemed to dwarf both of those combined.

To say the brown and red walls were deep would be an understatement. They were so vast and so deep that Sam thought he was looking at a crack into the centre of the planet. The distant walls appeared to be the edges of a super-continent. When he peered down out of the window, he saw the rocky colours darken and vanish into utter night.

It was beautiful and frightening at the same time.

To their right, the sandstorm raced towards them. To their left was the star Zanzia in the sky.

It would not surprise Sam if there were still pieces of rock in this gorge on which Zanzia's rays had never fallen. Nothing could be seen from the bottom of the gorge, for that the star was no longer high enough in the sky to cast its rays on it. The left side of the gorge cast darker shadows on the deeper parts. The slow blanketing of the shadow side was beginning to take control of the realm of day.

It was to that boundary between day and night that Ghala took the glider, deeper and deeper into the gorge, at what was a dizzying speed.

"Impressive," Sam had to admit.

"And this is just the first stretch," their guide said proudly. "With a depth of 438 kilometres U.T.S. and a length of more than three thousand kilometres, this is the most awe-inspiring place on this planet."

Tharo had seen bigger holes in the ground before, though. The gap on Trexlr, a world deep in the Quaat Empire, was more impressive. Nothing really impressed him anymore other than normal beings doing abnormal things.

"In about four minutes, we will arrive at the first bend, and there I have to reduce my speed. After the bend, we will have the shadow at our back and have a better view of what can be seen below."

Tharo felt that Ghala had given this touristy picture before, as if there was no approaching danger at all. To him, it was the answer to the question Sam had asked earlier, whether Ghala often transported people for some Digital Bell.

"How many turns are there?" asked Sam.

"Seventeen!" Ghala sounded enthusiastic.

They entered the bend of the gorge and for a moment, Sam felt as if the glider was going to crash against the shadowy side. Just in time, the glider's wings caught the air and they rounded the bend. Zanzia disappeared behind the rock face and the surroundings were suddenly turned inside out. They were plunged into darkness and even the heat inside the cockpit plummeted. Numerous headlights, both front and rear, together with the screen's night vision, automatically kicked in.

The shield also adjusted itself. It outlined the walls, the curve, the bottom, all the imperfections of the ravine around them in perfect digital overlay.

Deeper and deeper, they descended. At the next bend, Sam noticed how deep they were already and how much deeper they could still go.

At last, Sam understood what Ghala had meant when he said they would pass under the storm. It would rage over them without them feeling a thing.

Sam had a sense of pressure in his ears and he worried at them with his finger. Was it the speed they were travelling at or the depth? He looked down. Below them glittered a fast-flowing river that over the millennia had carved the ravine through the brittle rock. To his surprise, Sam also saw plants. Despite the scorching heat on the surface, down here where it was cooler, there were trees, some as tall as forty metres. They had long and narrow spindly deep green leaves that looked more like spikes than they did foliage. It was a peaceful oasis, an ecosystem unaware of the harsh world two hundred kilometres higher. Here, the gorge was wider and light reached the ground, enough for plants to flourish in a fertile environment.

At their phenomenal speed, they shot off towards a wall of light where the rock walls fell away left and right and where the river at the end of the gorge crashed below them in a crater so high and deep that the wind misted the water before it reached the bottom.

The glider rocketed out of the gap and Sam looked back. Before long, the gorge became nothing more than a crack in a towering wall. They had arrived at the centre of it all, a lake in an immense crater, which had to be more than a hundred kilometres deep. Above the lake, the steep walls still protruded for hundreds of metres.

"We will just barely make it," Ghala informed them after a long silence. "For a while, I thought we wouldn't but now I see we are going just a little faster than the storm after all."

"Why don't we just wait among the greenery until the storm passes?" asked Sam.

"This kind of storm can take days and you don't have that time," replied Ghala nonchalantly.

Tharo frowned a little as if considering something before brightening as he asked, "How big would this crater be? Four hundred and fifty kilometres U.T.S. wide? Five hundred?"

"Something like that," Ghala said, without taking his eyes off the lake.

"A crater of this size cannot be formed organically, either by a fast-flowing river or a natural disaster," Tharo continued. "An impact from outside could have been possible but you described this lake earlier as ruins. What occurred here?"

Sam curiously leaned forward. He didn't want to miss this answer either.

"True," Ghala said not without pride. "This was done by our predecessors, quite a few generations ago. The only and last time someone went in from the surface, which still inspires each of us to go on to the bitter end."

"And what, if I may be so bold," asked Tharo, "was that triumphant victory that still motivates your people today?"

"This was the largest city within the Underground network. Osthopat, they used to call it. But with the right equipment and a few go-getters, even the largest city in the Underground can be reduced to a painful scar on the surface of this planet."

It was difficult for Sam to imagine that the immense lake that lay below them had once been a bustling city. Its remnants, if there still were any, would be forever hidden under this body of water. He couldn't help but wonder if all this, what these terrorists were planning, was the right thing to do and whether or not they should help them achieve it.

"Was it a bomb?"

"A nanytobom-bomb," Ghala confirmed. "Inserted directly into one of the energy supply lines. The result was not optimal but it did wipe the city off the map."

"Was the destruction of an entire city with all its inhabitants not optimal?" Sam was bewildered and amused at the same time. He didn't think that any such large-scale disaster could ever be called "optimal" as if all of those lives were thrown away.

"Don't be so surprised," responded the moody Medotorian. "Their goal, and ours, has and always will be the annihilation of the entire Underground network. Its cities and all of the connecting tunnels must be destroyed in one fell swoop. If their plan had gone as planned then, and had the bomb been inserted into the fusion reactor that is connected with all the other reactors, then half the surface of Zanza would have consisted of craters and canyons like the ones over here."

Sam shuddered in horror. "Why didn't that happen?"

"Impossible to say. The rebels were caught or shot or managed to hold out long enough to go down with the city. Whoever takes it upon him or her to enter the Underground does so without any expectation of coming out alive."

Is that so? Sam thought. It seemed like the sort of thing that someone should have told him before.

The journey across the lake took longer than Sam had anticipated. It was more like an inland sea and when they had finally reached the far cliffs, Sam noticed that the storm had been hanging just behind them for some time.

Sam saw a waterfall in a crack in the wall in front of them, just like the one they had come out of earlier. The crack widened into a V-shaped chasm. The underground highways of this once grandiose city that connected it with all the others, Sam now knew.

Sam saw fine lines along the vertical walls and took a moment to realise what they were. "Pipelines?"

"For the farmers who supply all of Zanza with food, thousands of square kilometres of agriculture and livestock. Soon you will be able to see those up close," Ghala said.

Up close, the pipes were immense. The flow rate of water had to be enormous. Not surprising, Sam thought, with a star as scorching as Zanzia.

The moment the cloud made from glass and sand obscured the sun and threw the entire area into darkness, they shot into the green canyon. The glider immediately adjusted to the sudden lack of light. The storm wind behind them blew sand and glass into the crater, hitting the water and creating a racing edge of froth. Sam was glad that the most hazardous part of the storm still had several kilometres to cross before it would reach them. Sam got the impression that Ghala and Tharo had slightly exaggerated the storm. Apart from the slight hum of the engines, it was windless in the gorge and there was nothing to be seen of the nightmare they had passed.

After a while, they were out of the gorge and the deep darkness gave way to vast fields.

But...how does this exist down here? Sam's mind was blown at how this scorching planet could possibly entertain the acres of cultivated land he was seeing.

A shield? Sam thought. Was the farm using an energy field to withstand the heat of the weakened atmosphere – and presumably the storm that had crept over it? He wondered at the immense energy cost.

After a flight of what were thousands of kilometres and an inevitable diversion past the ruins, the lands of Ehben the Djockar finally came into view, an area of 750 hectares with residential and working buildings at its centre.

Ehben had specialised in growing two things. The first was Falaka, a crop about a metre high, rich in minerals, which, like all other things had been genetically engineered to survive in the scorching heat and with little water like the other crops. The second thing Ehben had turned to was the breeding of a livestock called Kiranas, eight-hoofed herbivores. They were giant mastodons from which a large family, if kept under the right conditions, could eat from for up to three months.

But as they approached Ehben's farm, what had looked like cultivated light brown and rich black squares of tilled earth changed in Sam's eyes. He wasn't seeing greenery. Maybe it was early in the Zanza season... or maybe it looked more and more like a dark patch in a white haze. Any healthy greenery had shrivelled into a white mass in the heat.

"The shields," Ghala said bewildered. "Why didn't they activate as the storm approached?"

"Maybe your Ehben didn't turn them on?" suggested Sam.

"Impossible. They are automated and have multiple emergency generators."

Meanwhile, the glider was already hanging low above the ground.

"When storms like these pass by, the shields should completely vaporise whatever substance lies on top of it. Something that clearly hasn't happened here."

Sam saw drifts of sands choking some of the beds, where the winds had clearly overwhelmed the sensitive biomes.

Tharo hummed. "You're right, something is clearly wrong here.

This is more than a technical glitch. Ghala, if I were you, I would ground the glider as soon as possible before someone catches sight of us."

"If it's not too late for that already," their guide agreed as he landed near the house among the remnants of Kiranas. The party stepped out and took a closer look at the animals. There was no trace left of their furry coats. Storm or no storm. Even in normal conditions, creatures like these had a light external fur which meant that were always protected by a shield of some fashion. Now, however, they had been sandblasted by glass racing past at hundreds of kilometres per hour. At the same time, inside the poor beasts, their blood had boiled until it had the consistency of caramel, spilling from their nose and eyes. After the storm had passed and the carcass had cooled, the mush had run out of the smooth carcass and dried around each beast into a thick, hard crust.

"This is not good," Ghala said. "I have never known it to be this quiet here, even without the sound of the animals."

"Did Ehben have a family?" asked Sam, looking around at the acres of destruction all around them.

"That's what worries me," Ghala said. "It was the children of Ehben and Rhynaiia who made sure it was never quiet here."

"The house is nearby," Tharo pointed out. He quickly added, "It might be better if I go ahead to assess the situation."

"No way," spoke the Medotorian. He walked back to the glider and took out a weapon from the rear boot, and another, and another, each one looking like a movie ray gun from Sam's memories of Earth. The last weapon was more rifle shaped and was almost as long as the Medotorian himself. "This havoc looks to me like it was caused by members of the LPF. If they are still there, I'll make them sorry soon enough."

Sam watched in amazement as Ghala did not hand out the weapons but hung them around his small body. "If you start shooting around, you also run the risk of destroying the map we came here for."

Ghala shrugged. "I don't think so. Ehben wouldn't just leave that map lying around in the open." He gesticulated around. "This calls for good old vengeance."

"First the map, then your vengeance," Tharo spoke sternly. "Don't forget that you, the rebels, need that map. If you start shooting at the officers inside, they'll shoot back first and only afterwards ask the necessary questions."

"Fine then!" sputtered Ghala. "Then we'll do it your way first. I'll give you ten minutes U.T.S., not a second more."

Tharo didn't have to tell Sam to stay with Ghala, they already knew each other that well.

Tharo disappeared among the cattle. Some of the carcasses had fallen so close together that the man had to squeeze through.

Ghala angrily threw pebbles at the nearest carcass that split open when it was hit a little too hard. The blood slowly dripping from it looked dark and viscous.

At first glance, the wooden house ahead of Tharo looked untouched. *So, at least the house's shield had apparently been activated*, he thought. The last rays of the sun setting in the storm on the horizon lit up the white-painted front facade, the porch, and the open front door. Everything else was covered in a dark layer of shimmering powder, including the countless barns and silos a little further on, and a playground to his right that the children no doubt used a lot. A fine, brownish dust hung in the air.

With a few creaking steps, Tharo walked onto the porch. He cast a first glance inside and...

"I hope for their sake there is an afterlife," spoke Ghala, who was the incarnation of stubbornness.

"I thought you were going to give me ten minutes?" remarked Tharo, without averting his gaze.

"I'm not exactly the most reliable Medotorian."

Sam, meanwhile, had joined them and did not manage to look away from the horror that had taken place inside. The nine bodies were tied up to a single beam. The first four looked young and lay clumped on the floor in the final throes of their agony. Tharo was convinced that the first two had never even opened their eyes. Djock-ar children only did that after two to five Méridian months, or two to five years U.T.S. after birth. It also remained questionable whether the next child had been able to celebrate the first six years of her life.

"Traces of LPF presence?" The Medotorian did his best to ask politely.

Tharo took a closer look at the smallest creature hanging half a metre above his head. "Looking at their state of decomposition, I think no one has been here for a long time."

The rotting children and the intense smell they secreted had no effect on the man.

Sam, on the other hand, was breathing through his mouth and had to restrain himself from gagging. While the two others went inside, Sam was left alone outside.

Of the two, Ghala was not bothered at all, especially since Medotorians did not possess a sense of smell. It was only the sight that made him a bit more hesitant. "It seems to me that Ehben himself hasn't been here yet, otherwise he would have already taken down their bodies."

"Which hopefully doesn't mean that he has fallen into their hands himself," Tharo pointed out.

Meanwhile, Tharo had averted his gaze from the nine victims and looked at the considerable havoc their killers had wreaked. "They must have been looking for the map very thoroughly." He disappeared into the next room. If the map was still in its hiding place, it couldn't have been large. Even the needles of a nearby clock had been removed to make sure there was nothing hanging behind them.

After about five minutes, Sam entered too, holding a hand over the lower half of his face. Of Tharo's and Ghala's presence, no more than a distant muttering could be heard.

The Medotorian had the impression that Ehben and Rhynaiia would never have left their children at home alone. Which meant that at least one of them was still in the house during the attack.

"Over here!" shouted Tharo from somewhere on the first floor.

For a moment, Sam felt hope that Tharo had found the map but that hope quickly went up in smoke as he reached the man. "Any idea which of the two this was?"

"Hard to say," he heard Ghala murmur.

With that, Sam could not help but agree. The room, decorated with a wall-to-wall soft mat like a relaxation or exercise room, was covered in congealed blood and pieces of body parts. "What on earth have they done here?" Sam whispered. He felt himself getting nauseous.

When Tharo opened the door, a piece of skull rolled away.

"Didn't you say something about the LPF not being so extreme?"

"Clearly not all of them are the same," spoke Ghala who, in the meantime, was crouching by one of the body parts. "I guess that you could say we must have seriously angered them for them to do something as foul as this. Anyway, I think this is Rhynaiia."

"How do you know?"

"They both have grey hair but Ehben's is darker and Rhynaiia's is silver-grey." He became more certain when he scraped off some of the blood caked around the hair with two fingernails.

"And to answer your question, Sam," Tharo spoke up. "I think they pointed a gun at her or plastered her with explosives."

"I need fresh air," gasped the pale Terran, who once more fled outside.

"I'll come with you and help you find some water if you or Ghala need it."

"There's some in the glider." Ghala called over his shoulder.

Immediately there was a dull, emphatic sound. It sounded as if someone was forcing the door and breaking into the house. Immediately, a deafening bang followed. The wooden house thundered. The explosion threw them all to the floor. Ghala was still crouched near the remains of Rhynaiia and fell straight into a large pile of rotting Djockar body parts. A second explosion followed, heavier than the first. The shock took the rear support walls with it. Again, another strike, this time much closer.

Dust filled the air, and the wall above Ghala and Tharo's heads burst inwards. Had Sam still been on his feet, he would have suffered more than a few scratches without Tharo's protection.

"Stay here!" shouted Tharo between salvos. He pressed the Terran against the floor and carefully straightened up.

Sam made no attempt to get up. His heart was pounding and his ears were ringing. A little further on, Ghala crawled forward across the floor towards the second stairwell at the end of the corridor. He was still covered in remnants of Rhynaiia and looked anything but happy.

Ghala took one staircase down, Tharo the other.

The latter had come to the conclusion that it was Ehben who was wreaking havoc. He based that on the fact that the assailant had tried to leave the entrance hall with the children's bodies unharmed. Another would not care what happens to a few Djockars who were dead anyway.

Downstairs, the havoc was incalculable. The place was a dusty mess and, in places, the wood from the walls was blown a metre high. Here and there, parts of the ceiling had also come down. There were holes in both the ground and first floors, and Tharo saw holes in the roof through which the sun's rays tried to bore through the thick cloud of dust.

When Tharo arrived downstairs, he found the lower part of the stairs in splinters. He jumped and came down onto the floor that began to creak under his weight. The noise, he realised, was easy for their attacker to hear. He glanced through a broken window and saw a single Djockar.

That Djockar, for his part, saw a Human, drew a quick conclusion, and just as quickly pulled the trigger of his weapon. Tharo, for his part, just let happen.

Still, there was a part of Tharo that flinched as the projectile went straight through his body. He startled but did not see or feel a single drop of blood while his smart clothes already started to fix themselves. His brain registered no pain because the nerves could not detect a wound. He was unhurt, and that was not lost on Ghala either.

The salvo that had passed through Tharo pierced three inner walls and exploded, creating a shock wave without a fire that *whumped* through the building.

"Ehben!" roared Ghala. "Stop shooting. There are only Freedom Fighters in this house!"

The silence that followed was interrupted only by the creaking of wood.

Finally, they heard shouting from outside. "Whose voice did I hear in there? Ghala? If it's you, come out or I'll keep shooting until not a shred remains of the house and your blue wrinkled skin! Ten seconds, no longer, you hear me?"

Ghala turned quickly to Tharo. "Stay here for now. Ehben's distrust of Humans is worse than mine." Then he turned to his friend outside. "Ehben! I may be blue but I'm still definitely wrinkle-free! Don't shoot!" Ghala started stripping off his weapons. "I'm coming out and I'm unarmed!"

Ghala straightened up. With his hands high up in the air, something that Tharo found slightly amusing, since his fingers didn't even reach the window for Ehben to see, he walked among the rubble towards the entrance. He was covered from head to foot in a thick layer of dust and walked past nine bodies swinging back and forth lightly.

Meanwhile, Sam had crept unharmed up to Tharo who, unlike Sam, looked at him standing upright. He had to ask him the question.

"Does this kind of lean towards what you imagined your whole Star Wars/Dune vibe to be like?" They both started grinning for a moment.

"I'm not going to answer that." Sam shook his head and stood up. He was thinking that this experience was a lot more *real* than anything he had ever imagined before.

"Not too badly affected?" Tharo asked.

"Scared, but strangely not one splinter or scratch."

"Then you have a thick skin," responded his mentor, taking a deep sigh and looking back towards the negotiations outside. Sam got the sudden impression that Tharo wasn't taking any of this that seriously at all. "This was your first encounter with a firefight. If we keep hanging around with the rebels, I doubt it will be your last. So, get ready."

Sam knocked the dust off his clothes which Tharo had allowed to pass through the shield to not make him suspicious. "Are you saying that I can use the cattaran?"

"If the local police forces are as aggressive with the residents down there as they are here, I'm pretty sure weapons won't be enough to get you out alive and well. You have my permission to use the cattaran, so long as you don't use it needlessly. Otherwise, you will be exhausted. The range of your flow is not limitless and your experience with the cattaran is still limited."

The flow, Tharo had told Sam long before all this, was the range of the cattaran. It was an undetectable form of energy emitted by the body. This energy had started developing when Sam was just a toddler. The older and more experienced he became with the cattaran, the greater the flow would become, and thus the range within which he could use it. He had tried several times to perceive it, like seeing a haze in heat overhead, but it was always without success. In other words, Sam knew that the more he trained, the better the results.

Pleased with the permission his mentor gave him, Sam turned his gaze back to the knotted-up children. He realised all too well what the Djockar had lost.

"By the way, couldn't you perceive Ehben inside the flow and just stop all this?"

"I did perceive him, or at least someone inside the flow coming closer, but I could not be sure who it was. It is unwise to unleash your power without wisdom," Tharo said firmly.

"People!" It echoed from outside. "I may be an old farmer but not nearly old enough to decide if I'm being messed with. Come out with your hands on your heads."

They did.

That the creature out there was indeed already of age was not apparent from it, even to a Djockar. He was wrinkle-free. Unlike other races, you can't tell the years of life of a Djockar just by the skin. It didn't get saggy and their health didn't get worse. Djockars were known to live long and prosperous lives. Outwardly, you could only tell Ehben's old age from his grey hair and his bones. On the inside, there was a unique process going on. An enzyme that occurred only in the bones of Djockars, accumulated over time, was turning his skeleton pitch black, causing it to shine through the skin. The process may have been a bone cancer but the Djockars themselves did not see it as a disease. The darker the bones, the more experience they had, and the more appreciation they got from the other Djockars.

Advanced science had created a cure for it out of the best intentions but that was not to the liking of the Djockar government, which had not been involved in the deliberations on this cure.

Arn, the Djockar bartender that Sam had met, was still quite young and had no visible skeleton. With Ehben, on the other hand, the dark skeleton was already quite visible, as Sam and Tharo saw as they approached. Where the skin tightened around the bones, the pale skin was dark.

"Ten murders for ten deaths," Tharo spoke with his hands on his head.

Sam saw that the Djockar, with his grey dreadlocks tucked back, looked slightly battered.

He looked at Tharo. Here and there, his skin, hair and clothing were covered in blood that Sam knew could not be his own.

"That' right," he sounded suspicious. "An old Djockar custom," Ehben did not lower his weapon and kept it pointed tightly at Tharo.

"Nine dead. Nine LPFs for my nine sons and daughters that did this and who I managed to track down. Their commander's heart for my other half, eaten with relish to ease my grief."

"Did it work?" asked Sam.

The Djockar now turned his cold gaze to Sam, who looked back calmly. "Not until we have destroyed the entire Underground and I use what remains of my existence to inflict as much damage as possible on the Administrator and his troops should they escape." The man spoke with conviction and hatred, and Sam didn't doubt he would attempt it.

Like Arn, Ehben's eyes were soulful, gleaming red and green.

"Then let us help you," Sam spoke.

The Djockars stern gaze seemed to wane for a moment and then refocused on Tharo.

"According to my little friend here, you are not Human. He says he saw one of my cartridges go straight through your body without even a scratch. He also said that if I didn't believe him, that I should just shoot you again."

"Ghala saw that right," Tharo said. "That would work on me but not on Sam here. So, if you try that on him, you would instantly be signing your own death warrant."

Ehben flickered a wary glance at the two newcomers but nodded, accepting Tharo's judgement. He signalled to the Humans to lower their arms.

Tharo continued. "We are all taking an enormous risk by being here and you know that all too well."

"You are not wrong about that," said the Djockar, with a glance at his nine children in the entrance hall. "Ghala also told me that you can be trusted and that I must not do anything to compromise this operation."

"So, the LPFs haven't found the map yet?" asked Sam hopefully.

"It was hidden in the safest place I could imagine," said Ehben, tapping his head with two fingers. "I heard you guys have something to retrieve files from a memory implant?"

Tharo nodded and pulled out his communicator. He opened the appropriate application and handed the device to the Djockar.

The latter operated the communicator as if it were his own. "I have tried everything to decipher the map but I have not succeeded yet. Therefore, I had decided it would be safer to store the file itself in an implant that was already in my head. I destroyed the original of the map and the duplicate is secured with a series of questions that only I can answer. Supposing I die, the file would be automatically sent to the oldest of my bloodline."

"Arn. Arn the bartender is your son, and that is why the LPF raided his bar!" Tharo suddenly realised.

"And the last real thing of value left to me," the old farmer nodded. He pressed the last key and a signal resounded. Ehben handed Tharo the communicator. "Send this to your ship as soon as the transfer is complete. I hope your Ship-Arti is powerful enough to crack the security. Otherwise, this was all for nothing."

THE GROUND ON WHICH WE STAND

Newly published article intended for Page Anonymous

The universe is vast, endless and ancient. Of all the life it has known so far, there were always only a few who could truly grasp the words used to describe the universe in its entirety.

For us to understand this grandeur, we must be able to imagine the size of Méridia. It is an ever-expanding object, a construction site, 1,657,339 km U.T.S. in diameter. A distance that can be covered by the lifts alone in about a Méridian month and a half, not counting the transit times from one lift to another, or the waiting times and stopovers. All the more reason, then, to do such trips outside by ship. The distance between this beating heart of Zan and Monstrosus, the black hole at the centre of Zan, is 1.5 light years or 1 Monster Astronomical Unit. A distance that can be covered by a ship in LDT, if it were allowed to, in no more than a few seconds.

Then again, with those same engines, such a ship traverses Zan at its widest stretch, from Red Line to Red Line, in about a hundred Méridian months. It is something few do, simply because there is no reason to. You can think of any inhabited space object as a neighbourhood within a megacity, with everything a normal citizen needs. Thus, there is no real need for a citizen to go into another neighbourhood. Entire families, communities, livelihoods and cultures exist out there in the depths of space, and the number of these inhabited space objects in our galaxy is like the drops of water in a sea. There are billions of them.

The largest migration ever was that of the Ferorians, of whom nothing has ever been heard since. Speculation surrounding their disappearance is endless. One of the most popular theories – and I cannot
believe I am getting this past my lips whilst speaking or writing all this
down – is that of the "One Galaxy For All" movement. The idea is that,
according to these simple creatures, we are in some kind of walled
sphere where all ships would just collide at LDT-speed, which is too
silly for words. Whether it is or not, I leave to your imagination.

Apart from that, of course, there are beings who in turn regard Zan
as a forbidden galaxy that is itself being watched but not entered.
So, according to them, what we do to the Forbidden Systems is being
done to us in the series, Ancient Worlds. Fortunately, we know better.

The Volgarians gave us LDT-speed and with their technology, the
doors of Zan opened wide. Shopping, working, ordering food or seeking entertainment in a nearby system is now at our fingertips. That
there was once a time when we spent years or sometimes centuries
travelling to neighbouring systems seems to have been forgotten by
everyone.

The longest-lasting Great War was one with the lowest number of
casualties, simply because the engines powering the ships were too
primitive and people ultimately became forgetful of why the war was
being fought in the first place.

Which brings me to my last point: time. That too is so obvious but nobody really thinks about it because, like distance, one simply cannot
grasp it. It is impossible to make it clear to the common man what a
billion Méridian years is on a cosmic scale. Therefore, to really grasp
time, a more tangible explanation is needed. When does fruit start rotting? After the first bite? After a planet's full rotation?

What do we consider to be "prehistoric"? We generally draw the
line at everything that takes place before the Volgarian Expansion.
Everything after that, we divide into Ages. Before that, there were only

the First Ones and the structures they left behind, which still prove indestructible to this day. People know that the First Ones existed, as their structures can still sometimes be found, and they are still just as indecipherable as they have always been.

CHAPTER 10

The cloud of ruddy brown and ochre dust hanging over the surface of Zanza was no mere consequence of the local weather. Within this wasteland of the northern region, some trick of the geography of the dying planet meant that there were almost no winds at all. It was still immensely hot but not nearly as hot as in the flat Zargan plains of Haraka. No, it was Ehben's glider that blew the dry dust up into the sky with all four thrusters, after which it came crashing back down into the dunes about a hundred metres away. Below the glider, a pit at least eighty metres wide and several deep had been formed, which Ehben had been working on relentlessly for the past seven hours.

Sam, under his heat-resistant poncho and with a supply of water, stood guard. He saw something approaching in the distance, a small dark shape on the distant horizon. He called out to Tharo and pointed it out. Tharo sat next to the pit in the sand and raised his thumb. He knew something was coming and had known long before Sam did, but he felt it necessary to give the Terran something to do.

The danger on the horizon soon grew into another glider, churning up the dust behind it in great billows, before it finally came to a halt next to the sand crater.

In it were Arn, Ghala, and two more strangers.

"For a moment, I thought you might not return," Tharo said.

"You weren't far off," said the Djockar. "The city is in turmoil because of the LPFs we made disappear. It took a while for us to get out of there undetected."

The two strangers, silently and without heat protection, started unloading some stuff from the glider.

"Then I just hope they didn't follow you," Tharo said heavily.

"No need to worry about that," Ghala reassured Tharo. "Disappearing undetected is something we Freedom Fighters have a lot of experience with."

Sam joined the trio and looked surprised at the two strangers. "Are these the only rebels you could muster?"

"The smaller the group, the more invisible we are," Arn said shortly. "Besides, there aren't many of us left now that the LPF has pretty much destroyed our bar and arrested whoever they could. If we fail, only those who stayed behind and managed to escape will still have a fighting chance with at least one of the two last bombs that Oni here made. We will have the other one with us.

Arn glanced at Ehben. The latter stopped the engines and looked up through the windscreen to where his son stood. Both Djockars nodded briefly at each other.

"Couldn't you have told us that Ehben is your father?" asked Sam.

"Irrelevant. Unlike you Humans, with us, a child's attachment to its parents is not nearly as close once it is old enough to leave home. Whether the reverse is also true, I won't know until I have children of my own. All that aside, it gives me genuine pleasure to see you again," the man said truthfully. "According to Ghala, getting here must have been quite an adventure." Arn beckoned the trio together.

Sam was the only one still paying attention to old Ehben, who was struggling to get out of the hole. For every step up in the loose sand, he sank back one and a half.

Arn continued, "Let me introduce you to the last two members of our little expedition group."

Sam looked away from Ehben and turned to the two creatures. He recognised the first one as a Crom, a creature that in the Terran's eyes looked most like a green-feathered bird crossed with a snake in some sinister experiment. It stood upright like a bird but its neck and head could have belonged to a snake, except they were covered in the same green feathers. Where Sam expected wings, there were long, delicate looking arms that it held behind its body. Sam could not discern any eyes, ears or nose, just a set of fleshy lips.

Arn pointed. "Oni here is our scholar. We owe the nanyto-bom-bomb to him."

The creature's thick lips parted in a wide grin. Behind it, Sam saw a couple of dozen hooked teeth. Sam had no doubt that these could impale whatever they could get their hands on in the blink of an eye.

The creature hissed, "I look forward to our little co-operation."

Sam got a strong impression that it was making fun of them.

Tharo, on the other hand, seemed unflappable. The creature tilted its head slightly and continued to keep its head towards Tharo. It was as if they were having a staring competition in which neither of the two would budge. Sam figured you didn't have to have visible eyes to give someone a piercing look.

Arn was already moving on and pointing at Oni's half-naked companion. "Inna here is our battering ram. Like all Olankans, you should expect no words, only growls."

Sam thought Inna looked even more intimidating than Oni, and that was saying something! Around his five broad arms, one of which came straight out of his chest and the other four at seemingly random points on his torso, the creature had hung a belt of weapons. On each of those weapons he held a giant hand, ready to draw. He was indeed somewhat like a battering ram, with his short legs, broad torso, and flat toad head. He was smeared with black and red paint, as if he had dressed for a final decisive battle in which he would intimidate all his opponents.

He growled kindly, or at least Sam got that impression that it was because of the tone.

Arn said proudly. "These two are of the best we have. Otherwise, I wouldn't have asked them to join us on this suicide mission."

"Suicide mission?" startled Sam. Once again, no one had thought to mention this particular fact to him.

"Not necessarily," Tharo reassured him, knowing full well that he couldn't change Arn's mind anyway. "There are ships down there that can take you straight back to the surface."

"Said the Human to a Djockar, a Medotorian, a Crom, and an Olankan," Arn pointed out, his tone caustic. It was as if they really believed that Humans were the only ones living down there. "Do you really think they'll let the rest of us non-Humans on board a ship? Or get off planet, even?"

Tharo did not address it. These creatures were so convinced they would die deep below the surface that there was no other outcome for them. Actually, if they would go in there, relaxed and without weapons between its residents, perhaps no one would even notice them.

Arn spoke then. "We are losing precious time." He pointed at Tharo. "Tell us about the map. Ghala said you were able to decipher it. Tell us, why exactly would we be able to find access to the Underground here and why this one in particular?"

"With pleasure." Tharo took out his communicator and looked at everyone.

"As to why this one in particular… I did tell you that we are here for business. At least for your people, it doesn't matter where you plant your bomb. The map you acquired is as old as the Subterraneans, and it hasn't been altered since then. A time when the Subterraneans were accessible to all. It has not been redrawn since then and we know this because the city you wiped off the map, all those generations ago, can still be found on it under the name Osthopat. All of the forgotten access roads from Osthopat to the Subterranean network are still shown on it."

"And according to the map, there is an access road here, under the sand dunes?"

"On the map, there is no desert at all," Tharo said as he handed Arn his communicator. "There are four more access tunnels hidden under the sand, stretching for eighteen kilometres under our feet to the subterranean levels. Maybe if you do survive this, it might be interesting for all of you exactly how this planet looked like before all this mess began. It was quite a paradise, back in the day."

With his fingers, Arn navigated the screen of Tharo's

communicator. "This is a strange network of corridors and rooms," he said hesitantly. He looked at a huge shaft on the map, which connected the surface all the way to the city below. There was a network of hundreds of rooms, stairwells and lift shafts. Everything spiralled around the main shaft to whatever could be found below. "Were these corridor systems created as emergency exits and entrances to the surface?"

Sam looked over his shoulder with him. "That's possible but I think the purpose of these corridors is simpler. You can't expand an underground city without bringing the earth from the new corridors back to the surface somehow, can you?"

"The company that hollowed out this subterranean world couldn't do that without first digging out shafts through which they could dispose of everything," Oni guessed. He turned his head towards Tharo, who looked approvingly.

The man replied. "This planet, as you all know, was not always a desert. I guess I shouldn't tell you what happened when the United Worlds of Man pulled the plug on Zanza? But while we're on the subject, here's an interesting fact about the sand we're standing on. Someone who approaches the Mining Guild with not a lot of natural resources and picks out a company to hollow out a planet can quickly regret it, as in the case of Zanza. The Systems that can afford it will therefore hire a company that takes not only the usable resources but also the unusable ones. Unfortunately, not every System can afford that. So, the sand we stand on, originally came from deep under our feet."

Oni also nodded now. "Through the shaft, they brought everything up, while all the rest was used as living space for the tens of thousands who worked on it."

"The lower the quality of the company, the less automation they deploy for such jobs," Ghala nodded sagely. He seemed to be speaking from experience. "Without the necessary comforts and with the long duration of such jobs, you risk workers dropping out of work before starting the actual job. I have already seen that go wrong with my own eyes."

"Are you guys done babbling?" shouted Ehben from below. He had given up on climbing and glared up at them.

Everyone looked at him. With a good sense of timing, the old Djockar held a spade and stuck it deep into the sand. The sound of metal on metal echoed.

For hundreds, maybe even thousands of Human generations, it had been dark and still inside the elevator shaft beneath Arn's feet. Suddenly, a spark appeared. The searing flame of Arn's cutting torch made its way through the thick metal gate like a hot knife through soft butter. Gobbets of molten steel dropped from the roof, hissing as they disappeared into the darkness. Soon, Arn had carved out a section a metre by a metre, falling into the darkness beneath it. The shaft was so deep that they would have to wait quite some time to hear the heavy metal touch the ground.

They heard a hiss.

Arn flinched. "How likely do you think it is that there is anything alive down there?" he asked Tharo. Without essentials like food, light and oxygen, nothing could survive there, it seemed to him.

"Well, there are more than enough creatures like the Volgarians who can perfectly thrive in conditions where others cannot." Tharo looked into the hole and saw that the walls of the shaft were filled with remnants of scorched foliage. "Unless you're talking about more than just complex life." The plants had to have been scorched in the light of the cutting torch.

From under his clothing, Tharo pulled out a glass, a piece of broken-white marble. He squeezed it for a moment in order to add a little bit of pressure and then dropped it.

Everyone bent over the hole and waited for something to happen. The marble emitted a bright light that set the foliage lower down the shaft ablaze as it fell down. Everyone, not counting Tharo, flinched. The burnt-up foliage hissed and crackled.

Oni nodded. "The plant of Nimbas. A climbing plant that can only survive in total darkness."

Inna growled.

"Heard a lot about it already but never seen it in real life. The plant is extremely sensitive to light." Oni continued, "and the smoke is extremely poisonous."

"We have air filter masks that adjust to the wearer," Arn replied, "and I suggest we use our night vision goggles."

Tharo, waving away the mask he was offered, looked down the shaft again now that the burning had stopped and only the faint light of the marble shone on the bottom that only he could see. "I estimate it goes down here about 2.5 kilometres. But I highly doubt the lift is still working."

"Don't worry, we are equipped," said the Medotorian.

Inna put down his pack.

"For me too?" asked Sam, as he was painfully aware that at least one Human on the team was not immortal.

Arn nodded. "I take care of everyone."

Tharo nodded. "Then we'll meet down below." Before anyone realised what his intentions were, he jumped into the dark opening without any rope or security.

Arn, shocked, stepped back as Sam started smiling.

"Does he really have no fear of death or is he just absent-minded?"

"He simply can't die," said Sam matter-of-factly.

"Right..." said Arn hesitantly, taking a second suspicious look down the hole from which no anguished screams or mortal thumps had yet been heard. "Ghala had already said something like that." He turned to his father. "Ehben, you go down first. Age before charisma and all that."

—

The night vision goggles gave Sam a masterful view down the long and wide shaft where, once, several elevators would have moved up and down in order to dispose of the excavated earth and rubble. He saw that Ehben had already arrived at the bottom, looked up and disappeared. Arn had hung Sam on a fine, extremely strong, intelligent rope and so he descended slowly. Along the walls, the Nimbas plant still smouldered. At the slightest touch, charred leaves, flowers and stems tumbled down. At the bottom, Sam saw the light that Tharo had thrown in the shaft. As he got closer to it, the night vision goggles automatically adjusted and the rope automatically began to slow down.

The old Djockar was already walking towards him to untie him. Sam let him, having no experience of it himself. Ehben lifted him like it was nothing. Useful information about Djockars, Sam thought, was that they were immensely strong even when they were old.

"Isn't Tharo here?"

"He's already gone ahead," the old Djockar said after setting Sam down. The rope disappeared even more swiftly than it had come. "Feel free to look around yourself, it will be some time before we are all down."

Ehben stayed by the light source waiting for the next person to descend the shaft.

It was only there that something of the original floor could still be seen, cobblestones spaced far apart. Around the bottom of the shaft, the Nimbas had burned away but deeper down the corridor that led to the lift entrances, the vegetation grew luxuriantly.

Soon, Sam could detect nothing of the light. Here, in this total darkness, the usually blood-red plant thrived best. Not one piece of wall in this underground tunnel network had remained uncovered. Under his feet, Sam felt a network of thick branches. He would have to watch where he walked in the thick fog of gases released by this noxious weed.

Here in the corridor, the ceiling was twenty metres high. If he had wanted to, he could have climbed up over the Nimbas in no time. Left and right in the walls were openings, access holes with more corridors, and rooms behind them for the tens of thousands of workers employed here at the time. Now it was empty and overgrown. As he squinted, the overgrown entrances sprang into clarity as his goggles showed him every detail. He saw bunk beds as high as five beds, washrooms, dining tables and chairs, all of them surrounded and covered by the creeping Nimbas.

After about five minutes of exploring, he gave in to his sense of apprehension and wanted to return to the others. He found Tharo standing in the overgrown doorway.

"This is a special plant," said the latter. "It uses darkness as its main food source and needs only minimal water and oxygen to survive. All of this from just one seed that, who knows, may have been brought here in the pockets of a worker." He saw that Sam was not paying attention. "Everything all right?"

"No idea," Sam admitted. He searched for words to make his feelings clear. "On the Dévara, you once talked about being able to sense others with the cattaran?"

Tharo's eyes burned into him. "So, you feel it too."

"You too?"

Tharo moved closer to Sam, hands behind his back. "Ever since we came out of the LDT," giving Sam an immediate idea of how immense the man's flow must be. "It's like we're not alone here. You'll get used to the uneasy stimuli that come with that."

"What does this mean for us?"

"Nothing."

"Nothing?" Sam thought to himself. On Terra, he had caused enough suffering to the bounty hunters to make it difficult for any adversaries here. When he allowed his mind to still, or he grew bored, he was struck by the most frustrating sensation that he and Tharo were not alone; had never been alone, in fact, since they had arrived in the Zanzia system. It was almost like being watched – only it wasn't.

Sensing his rebellious thoughts, Tharo said, "There are two kinds of Cattarians. Those who can camouflage the cattaran and those who cannot. Above all, try to concentrate on the here and now." He started walking back to the rest of the team and Sam followed. "Keep your emotions in the background but don't lose sight of them. We must not forget that we are here for a purpose. Whoever it is we feel is still far enough away from us. So, keep the cattaran inside camouflaged until it is absolutely necessary to use it."

"Sam! Tharo! Are you coming?" Arn's voice, the group leader, echoed through the corridor.

"Concentrate on the here and now," Tharo repeated. "We have more than a day's walk ahead of us before we reach the Subterranean. After that, we'll see what happens."

THE GREAT EQUALISATION

Newly published article intended for Page Anonymous

I have referred to it on several occasions. Written about it in previous publications and in sometimes quite a lot of detail. The Great Equalisation. Let there be no doubt about it, it was a historic moment in our Zanese history but one with such far-reaching consequences that they can still be felt to this day.

I recently overheard a conversation between two Zanese individuals on exactly this but I have to say, more misinformation was exchanged rather than actual facts! History, with all our media on hand, has never been so close and accessible. But it is a history that, if taken from sources other than the Zan Chronicles, may well be highly distorted. Again, those interested in, well, all subjects of life and beyond are best to turn to the Zan Chronicles. I'm not paid to say this, it's just the way it is. I thought, therefore, that with all the problems today, it might be interesting to revisit that same topic.

So, what was this monster project called the Great Equalisation? Well, it was definitely one of the longest-lasting undertakings in the entire history of Zan. It was the beginning of something big. A first step of many towards that other historical event that was known as the Golden Age. Or, in other words, that Utopia that has long existed here in Zan and was itself in turn a part of another, much more bombastic, kind of plan that involved more than just Zan. That is all I will say about the latter which YOU, the reader, will never again hear about or at least not from me. What I can say about that, however, is that after the fall of the Utopia in which we found ourselves, the Age in which Zan and its inhabitants were at their best, in my opinion, was never fulfilled.

Now, back to the subject at hand. The Great Equalisation. The idea or theory behind it was simple. Zan, at the time of the Volgarians, began with a single species (namely those same Volgarians). It was, and still is, a species that was interested in nothing more than observation and the accumulation of knowledge, always maintaining an aloofness in the millions of U.T.S years during and after the Volgarian Expansion. Under their observing eye, one species after another slowly but surely appeared on the scene, and they eventually brought with them much violence. However, long after all those conflicts between the emerging interstellar species, at a meeting organised by the Volgarians (which was named Zantmoet), a delegate from each Territory made their appearance. A delegate for each of the 299 pieces into which Zan was divided, belonging to the 299 species that had each appropriated a piece of space. Some species owned no more than a few hundred planets while others had many thousands with many billions left untouched and uninhabited.

(And in case YOU as a reader were wondering whether or not I was there, the answer is yes. Maybe I should leave that to your imagination and also say no.)

A lot of Ages later on yet another Zantmoet, out of the 299 species, only 163 remained. Many disappeared through war, others through disease, poor equipment, poor technology, or simply a lack of habitable planets. The great filter, which allowed some civilisations to pass through and others not, was merciless. It was the Volgarians who came up with the idea that, if things continued as they were, it would, over time, turn disastrous for everyone in Zan. Life as it stood now, they felt, was far too weak.

Besides, an entire species should not be allowed to disappear just because it is short of something and ends up having no option but to take it from those who, in some cases, have far too much. I am obviously talking about those same resources such as natural minerals, renewable energy, and of course, water. A lot like the situation we have today, you might say.

There was a shortage of habitable planets. It was the Volgarians who believed that all that should not be obtained from another but rather be obtainable in not just any territory but anywhere and at any time in Zan.

All that aside, 163 space-faring species, and everyone agreed on that, were far too few to make all that possible and so those same Volgarians took it upon themselves to take on an immense task. In other words, there was quite a lot of tinkering with genetic material to make life possible on other planets. What exactly that tinkering entailed or how it was achieved, well, there's nothing about that even in the Zan Chronicles.

So, what did the Great Equalisation consist of, that event that would not have been possible without the Volgarians?

Step one: The creation of habitable atmospheres in places where that was not possible before.

To date, more than 90% of all life forms require an atmosphere similar to that of the newly-added planet of Terra. This meant that billions of planets, regardless of their distance from their star, if possible, had to be made habitable. In addition, they had to be supplied with just the essential minerals to make the next steps possible. To accomplish this immense task, the first Guilds were introduced from somewhere within what is now the United Territories, consisting of numerous companies dedicated to achieving these ambitious goals.

Step two: Life would no longer be peculiar to a single planet.

Thanks to genetic engineering and a lot of cross-breeding, a cosmic exchange of life was triggered. Like an explosion, animal and plant species were deliberately dispersed by travellers and planted where necessary on countless planets, making Zan home to a diversity of life forms. From Kiranas to exotic flora, thanks to the Great Equalisation, Zan became a vibrant patchwork of biological splendour and wonders.

Step three: The Volgarian promise.

In no less than twenty U.T.S millennia, life was thriving in all of its many forms.

It is believed that the Volgarians had spread a chemical cocktail whose recipe has never been deciphered to this day. A task that was later given to the World-Building Guild. Its purpose was to add more intelligent species to the 163 others that had approved the Great Equalisation, and they succeeded.

Dear readers, before you wonder whether or not you are the product of their contribution, try not to worry because you will likely never find out. Many have tried and all have been left with nothing but questions. Just because your planet was made habitable doesn't mean that your species was put together by the Volgarians. It is important to know that not every species originated this way. Many thousands arose on their own original, habitable planets.

Anyway. The prediction that the Volgarians had made about the dangerousness of evolution has been proved right. Of the 299 original species present at the very first Zantmoet, after a few hundred million U.T.S. years, only eight of them remain today: the Volgarians, Humans, Thurrock, Djockars, Quaats, and Sollomon each still have their own Territories within the now Remaining Ten. There are also the oft-forgotten Hyossas that united the United Territories and the Bactalla inside the Neutral Zone that some say are even rarer than the Volgarians. Along with those same Volgarians and the Thurrock, they are presumably also well on their way to disappearing forever.

However, it is clear that the Volgarians delivered in their promise to re-seed the galaxy. There are as many as 692 009 diverse space-faring species that are so spread out that there is no longer an extinction crisis.

Step four: Technology

A project as big as the Great Equalisation could not be realised or even maintained without the necessary technology, and the Volgarians were the main contributor to that. They shared whatever they found necessary to ensure the Great Equalisation. Not only their planetary engineering techniques but also Arti technology, among others, which were introduced to enhance fragile life with countless implants. Ships were equipped with LDT-generators, the Galactic Net appeared, and all the applications that followed. All of that and so much more we owe solely to the Volgarians.

But what were the consequences within today's society and how did all that then lead to the fall of the Golden Age?

Quite simply put, despite the great flourishing of life that the Golden Age brought, it also brought with it a great burden of care, resources, and cost. Virtually all the planets that were once so inhospitable to life needed immense care, and such care involves immense resources. Providing energy is not really a problem thanks to the Memtrasts and everything connected to it but that too requires immense maintenance and those things are not exactly cheap. They can provide a planet with a shield but that is not nearly enough. In fact, it is all the rest that causes the planets to slowly but surely wither away until such a time as there is nothing left to be seen of the Great Equalisation.

If you doubt my words, then, wherever somewhere in the Cosmos you are reading this, you probably shouldn't look far to see such a planet with your own eyes. Calla, Zoptotto III, Zanza, Ra, and Earth are just a few examples of worlds where the population is literally withering away, either from overheating or from a biting cold, or from the dis-appearance of the atmosphere. The more prevalent it becomes, the more tension there will be until eventually all we will know is war, starvation, and death.

I know, cheery, aren't I?

I say this not to scare you but to wake you up. When all of this is no longer sustainable, those living at the end of the Great Equalisation will look back at those who started it and will do so with a certain hatred and jealousy. A simple spark would be all that is required to blow the entirety of Zan apart.

So, hold on tight. For it will get much, much worse.

CHAPTER 11

```
Zan: 1983, 55th A.o.Z., a.V.E.

Monster-Méridia Calendar: 1.05.024;

Méridia-Archive Calendar: 2.18;

Terra (UTS): 2628.08.16

Zanza, Zanzia System, Sattar Province, The United
Worlds of Man, Gamma A, Third Circle, Zan
```

met Rhynaiia when she came knocking on my door looking for work," Ehben told them. "Months after her ship had to make an emergency landing."

The group walked down a pitch-dark corridor and listened to Ehben's story. Sam's breathing was heavy inside the filter mask he wore as the thick gas of the Nimbas plants hung around them. Tharo and Arn walked in the lead, with Inna behind. From the group, Tharo was the only one who was walking around without both a breathing mask and night vision goggles. Within the flow, he had told Sam that he could see and even feel things that no one else could. For the others, it was an experience that seemed to have quite an intimidating effect, and they didn't dare ask questions.

"She was so different then, more ferocious. She was far from ready to start a family. Not surprising. Young Djockars at that age find it more important to become Zan's best warriors."

"Is there nothing, then, that a Djockar would shy away from?" asked Sam, walking beside the old man.

"Of course, there is. But fear and anger are emotions you can, with proper training, simply turn on and off when things get serious," Ehben said with an air of experience.

Inna growled.

Oni interpreted that as, "He's saying, 'wait till you measure up to a Quaat, or an Olankan like Inna.'"

Ghala added: "A Satankan is not to be underestimated either."

Oni parried: "Quaats are raised as warmongering creatures and have already developed muscle mass in their Armour when they hatch. Satankans, Djockars, and Olankans do not. A Quaats' advantage on the battlefield is strength, intimidation and a virtually impenetrable Armour. A Djockar is also made for battle but what they lack in strength, they make up for in speed and agility."

Ghala gave a displeased sound. Sam wondered if this was species rivalry.

"The Champions of Zan," Oni continued, "are won six times out of ten by a Quaat."

"But if it is not a Quaat who wins," Ehben interfered in the conversation, "he is eliminated by a Djockar. A Quaat can win a fight with a single blow but they are slow and don't think about tactics. Besides, they need meat to make their Armour work optimally. The longer without meat they go, the more likely they are to lose."

"Quiet now!" hissed Arn from twenty metres away with Tharo, near the end of the corridor.

Only then did Sam notice that the foliage had become less dense. At the end of the tunnel that curved sharply to the right, they saw a whitish glow.

Sam, following the actions of Ehben and the rest, pushed up his mask and night vision goggles. It was light enough to discern his hands and fingers.

"At last," Ehben whispered, and the group stepped forward into the forbidden underground city.

Their very first impression of the subterranean realm was not what they had imagined. They were standing on an old, unused maintenance ledge some two hundred metres long, which disappeared to the left and right into the distance. After the dark light in the corridor, they now found themselves in a shadowy cavern.

Tharo and Arn were already standing near the edge and gazing down. A thick layer of dust carpeted the ledge, disturbed only by their footprints.

Sam cast a glance over. From afar, he could see that the pillar that stretched from the bottom to the very top of this huge cave, which had no doubt held together for millennia. The city itself, which lay about a kilometre and a half below them, was built into a descending spiral, in which the structures were cascading. The tallest stood against the cliffs and looked to be about two kilometres high. The adjacent buildings were about ten or twenty metres lower, and so they went down and down to the centre, where in the pillar lay a vast arena. That was where Sam and Tharo had to go.

Dirty, sooty apartment buildings stood close together as if they were one, consisting of countless sparse small residential units. The centre was hidden behind a dark smog cloud, the result of air filters that hadn't worked for centuries.

Ghala was the first to find his words. "For twenty-five Méridian Thirds, I used to believe that they lived like kings and queens in here. But now I cannot help but feel pity. Their situation here is more dire than ours. You told me, Tharo, you told me but I didn't listen. I guess I just couldn't. What happens to one happens to another. The United Worlds of Man, I see now, abandoned not only the surface but the entire planet."

"I don't get it," Arn said. He looked at Tharo. "Why would the billions of inhabitants in the entire Underground prefer dark holes such as these to a life on the surface? With the right technology, they could learn to live with the heat."

"Because some minds simply aren't capable of adapting. All across Zan, people cling to their traditions and their beliefs, wishing that things will get better or some miracle will occur. No one is willing to admit that the glory of Zan is fading," said Tharo.

The others nodded. Zan was letting down not only everyone on the surface but now everyone in the underground cities as well.

Not surprisingly, Sam was the first who had accepted this idea and asked a simple question. "How are we supposed to get down there?"

Ehben looked at the thousands of gliders skimming between the buildings in the dark veil above the fog. The city was inhabited, clearly, and there was movement and light happening across the space below them.

How many people lived there? Sam thought. It had to be thousands. Tens of thousands.

"We should get one of those up here," Ehben grunted.

"I have an idea," Sam said. Some distance away, dusted crates were piled up. Sam concentrated, and felt the quiver of energy inside of him.

The cattaran.

Easy now, he counselled himself, breathing in steadily. He remembered his teaching on board Tharo's ship, reached towards that energy coiled inside of him, and coaxed it like he would a feral cat.

Sam thought of his past. Of all the times he had been scared and the cattaran stirred, leaping towards the surface. He sent the power flinging towards the crates...

In an instant, the whole pile began to shift to the edge with a loud groan. The freedom fighters looked in awe when Sam, with an outstretched hand, pointed at the stacked boxes. They shifted faster now and fell over the edge, facing the busy traffic. A plume of dust followed the crates, slower.

Tharo said dryly: "One would probably have sufficed too."

Sam and Tharo looked down, while the others just couldn't help themselves and kept staring at Sam. A few seconds later, they saw the gliders below abruptly swerve and come to a halt. A glider was making its way up to them.

Sam gestured to the others to quickly hide. "They might get suspicious at the sight of so many weapons."

The rest of the group hurried back to the concealing darkness of the corridor, just in time for the glider's lights to pierce their ledge, and then the vehicle itself appeared, turning and delicately landing a little way from Sam. A burly Human stepped out, wearing deep green and blue fatigues. "How did you manage to get so high above the city?" The man rubbed his long beard.

"Long story," Sam shrugged.

The man's eyes grew big as he saw the little Ghala appear with a very big gun.

"A Medotorian? Here? Well," the Human chuckled nervously, "Now I've truly seen everything." Before the man realised what was about to happen, however, Ghala had already pointed his weapon at him. It was a huge quiver, which seemed even bigger in the Medotorian's minuscule hands. He pulled the trigger and the man disintegrated. Or rather, partially. What was left of him flew over the edge into the depths. All that was left were a pair of steaming shoes.

"Was that, uh... really necessary?" Sam whispered, only for Ghala to sneer back.

"Ask that of Ehben, who just lost his entire family!"

Meanwhile, the others had also emerged.

"Heavy artillery," considered Tharo.

"The heavier the artillery, the bigger the damage," Arn said practically.

Tharo thought *They're just little boys with guns that are far too big.*

"As long as you know what you're shooting at," Tharo said. "That nanytobom-bomb of yours is not the only thing here that can say boom and the closer to the core you go, that risk will only increase."

"Who wants a lift?" asked Ghala, who was already casually standing on the glider's ladder, ignoring Sam who, after having seen how the man disappeared before his eyes, was taken aback a little. He slowly breathed in and out to calm down.

—

"So, we have our way down," said Tharo after taking a seat while he took out his communicator. "We will get out near the closest ridge and I suggest that is where our paths separate. Sam and I have our own plans, and not much time is left for us." He pointed to a spot on the map where Ghala could drop them off. "We'll find transport to the arena from there."

Arn looked at another spot on the map. "For us, it's going to be a whole lot trickier. The main reactor we want to go to is in the most central point of the city and can only be reached through the sewers. The normal entrance is far too heavily guarded. We'll never get through there."

"Complexes with such a large drainage grid will no doubt have some kind of transport system for the maintenance crews," Ehben considered.

Arn had prepared the mission thoroughly. "True. There is a network of guided vehicles. All you have to do to use them is enter a location. Then again, the problem with that is that the LPFs can also stop them remotely."

"Leave that to me," Oni said calmly.

"It is precisely for these kinds of situations that I asked you to come along, Oni." Arn's short tone put an end to counterarguments. He zoomed in on the map and looked at Sam and Tharo.

No one asked any more. The mission, with the resources they had, had been thoroughly gone through beforehand and any unexpected problems would have to be solved on the spot. Even with their preparations, it was clear to Sam that no one expected to see each other alive again.

"We'll each go our own way," Tharo said. "As long as we get enough time to do our thing."

"Are you doubting my bomb-making skills?" asked Oni defensively.

"No," Sam soothed. He hoped.

"That is completely unjustified," the Crom continued. "Only the injector can stop the bomb but it destroys itself after the Artis have been inserted. Once injected, the process is irreversible but rest assured, it will take several hours for them to say 'boom'."

Arn knocked the dirt off his clothes. "Let's go and get this done then!"

THE DANGERS OF ONLINE DATING IN THE COSMOS, PART 3

Newly published article intended for Page Anonymous

Missing person announcements. I speak for everyone when I say that they can be seen everywhere. On the Ack, it was mostly children's faces looking at me from numerous walls, sent in automated messages or projected sometimes over entire cities. Only we all know that these young people aren't really young at all, don't we? That is what makes this situation so tragic.

Here's the thing. It is actually recommended to start the astrazan only when you are an adult. If children take the astrazan, then childhood is unnaturally prolonged. Imagine your child is a century U.T.S. in nappies and has yet to learn to talk and walk but also has an adult mind. Imagine spending years with an adolescent in the house.... Normal puberty lasts long enough already. With the Artis that regulate the astrazan, it can last at least six to ten times longer which, depending on the species you belong to, can then be extended by years. Perhaps the sorriest part of taking the longevity drug is that once you start taking it, you cannot stop. The withdrawals and sudden ageing can kill you. For my part, I believe that the astrazan should only be taken when the person in question is ready.

I understand that it is difficult for those parents to be stuck with a young, needy child for centuries. Of course, few parents willingly kick their child out of the door, even if they are centuries old! But it does happen. There is only so long that a parent's loving patience can last, as they say. Often enough, these adult children are abandoned or they themselves run away from home. They turn up in another system, another province, or even another territory. The chances of them coming back to their parents are slim.

The step to crime is a small one. This poses numerous ethical problems. Can you still speak of child soldiers or child labour or abuse when the child in question is over a century U.T.S. of age and as intelligent as an adult? Not every territory tries these children as adults, allowing them to get away with more crimes. Numerous ships are raided by gangs composed solely of seemingly young people. The most dangerous are not the apparent youngest, it has to be said. Those stuck in their teenage years are generally used as lookouts, spies, or thieves. It is the older-seeming ones, the ones without a blush of grey or wrinkle to their skin yet, who are the worst. They can hold an engaging conversation. They are the epitome of social desire.

Which brings us back to the Ack, an unremarkable, shall we say, mini-between-station where many of these so-called poor bastards end up. A place in the deep vacuum that partly serves as the base of The Silver Moon, an organisation that deals exclusively with the victims of all those dating sites I mentioned in my earlier posts. Child or adult, these cruel individuals in young bodies are part of a well-oiled machine that have faced no opposition for years. Until now. Because now, Mister Blex is here.

I am here to inform you, dear reader, that many of those responsible in the Silver Moon may look like angelic youths, like supermodels or actors in their second decade of human normal age, but they are in fact far older, and addicted to astrazan. They use their apparent innocence as a lure.

Those who choose to live in the great vacuum know well enough that the horror may be closer than you think. For these adult youths within The Silver Moon, I am that horror. To them, I am a Demon, a nickname

I have also heard from Jara and the Artis inside Shoba's information about our kind in their communications. There is an organisation that calls itself the Changelings. Coincidence? We will fully peruse the files in their central computer and then we will know.

One thing has become immediately clear to me: what these preternatural youths are doing here is bound to shock. The thousands of victims who sought contact with strangers through apps and websites were brought here by members of The Silver Moon and kept in cells. I have already walked past those cells. I can tell you, I have seen and done a lot of lurid things but what happens here is sickening.

A woman hung chained to the wall with both arms above her head. In front of her on the floor were her own rotting intestines. If I were anyone else and, moreover, not in possession of emotion blockers, it would have been a traumatic experience that would have sent me straight to the many understaffed support groups.

All those victims and to think that all they were looking for was someone who could love or help them.

What will Blex do now? I think, dear reader, that by now you already know. I run organisations like these to the ground. Rosa, this is for you. And that brings us to the end of our series concerning the dangers of online dating in the Cosmos. Now, whether they look innocent or not, I will make sure that justice prevails and that there is no one left to tell the tale...

Only then will I bother to contact the Guardians.

THE ZAN SPACE GAMES

Newly published article intended for Page Anonymous

The Zan Space Games are an event that takes place only once every five Méridian years and lasts a mere twenty weeks U.T.S. A spectacle full of fame and glory that of course makes the ISSA, the Interplanetary and -Stellar Association for Sports-related Activities, which organises these Space Games, obscenely rich.

It is one of the few things that can still captivate me in this long life of mine. Well, that and writing these anonymous posts, for which I am immensely grateful to the moderators behind Page Anonymous. My family may be of the opinion that I am not doing the right thing, throwing all this, my life and opinions, onto the Galactic Net but I enjoy doing it. So let the risks (hello Guardians of Zan) be damned. The disciplines inside the Space Games are numerous and, with the exception of the youth events, are played without the use of holographic simulations. In other words, those who mess up don't always return for the next edition.

In the first week, it was the weightless divers who faced the most extreme obstacles, interspersed with the daredevils in the GLDRs. This week, week two, it's the disciplines of downhill sports on comets, meteorites, or the planets whose peaks reach high into the atmosphere. The more extreme, the better. For this spectacle, I sometimes get out of my lazy seat aboard the Krom to wallow in enthusiasm and booze in one of the M-pubs.

I have always loved observing an event like this with the common plebs. Sport is something that brings species together, whatever their relationship. I saw a Quaat cheering for a weightless diver at the same table as a Medotorian, a Djockar, a Human and a Sprall. It was the Human, an old, gritty female, who shouted loudest of all. Old, but clearly young at heart, as it turned out.

It was that same woman who addressed me at the bar a few days ago. Her name was Babs and she was hoping to make her move. I do enjoy seeing anyone enjoying themselves but declined her offer. I told her that I had been looking forward to this event for too long, and that I intend to observe the full twenty weeks. Babs found it strange to see me sitting on the same stool day in and day out, but eventually she would become sort of a bar mate of mine.

CHAPTER 12

Zan: 1983, 55th A.o.Z., a.V.E.

Monster-Méridia Calendar: 1.05.024;

Méridia-Archive Calendar: 2.18;

Terra (UTS): 2628.08.16

Zanza, Zanzia System, Sattar Province, The United
Worlds of Man, Gamma A, Third Circle, Zan

Standing next to Tharo in the crowd on the landing pad, Sam watched the glider packed full of Zanza freedom fighters fly away. He doubted that he would see any of them ever again.

They stood at the highest point of the subterranean city proper, having descended their original access ledge to one of the bustling landing platforms that overlooked the metropolis below. Gliders came off and on in a constant dance. Underneath this top floor hung two more ledges on which trade was done round the clock. This highest platform was now swarming with people, a mixture of species but the vast majority of them were Human.

From here, Sam could see multiple holographic screens showing the highlights of T750C, Tharo's Arti. Those same highlights, Tharo had already observed, had also been seen circling in and around this system over social media. The crowd cheered at the sight of their champion's heroics. It was clear they were looking forward to his twentieth fight.

They chartered a taxi driver to the arena and got in. Now that they had lost their company, of whom some were armed to the teeth, the two Humans blended into the crowd more easily.

The closer they got to the centre, the lower the buildings became. Each structure was divided into eight blocks, separated by a wide street. Across the small alleys and wide intersections, Sam could discern aerial bridges, one above the other, stacked and looking like some maddened mechanical spider had made its endless metal webs across the city. Sam looked back. The platform they had just left was already beginning to look murky through the dark veil of smog. He turned around again. In front of them stood a pillar, lit up by three horizontal lines with four red flashing lights to each.

Once on solid ground, Sam got up close and personal with the smog, which was denser here lower to the ground. It smelled of heavy metals and Sam could taste them in the back of his throat. The pillar in the city centre towered over them for kilometres but because of the dense smog, Sam could only see the bottom fraction of it. At the bottom of the pillar, a mass of spectators streamed inside, all of them on their way to the arena. No one looked back at them.

"Let's go," Tharo spoke. He pulled Sam into the stream of enthusiasts. "We have some time before the festivities start here. More than enough time to see the main event."

Inside, it was less dark than outside. They entered the arena part of the pillar through a twenty-metre corridor. Sam was reminded of the Colosseum of ancient Rome. The corridor sloped up to a wall with hundreds of lifts, the only access to the arena.

There was no guard, no one to seat them, and no one to whom they could turn for information. No one alive, anyway. There was a system connected to all sitting and standing areas, and the lifts only took them to an underground floor where there was still room and from which available seats were lit up with certain colours. Sam, reading only one rule about this system, found it interesting how each and every spectator had to respect the seating colour assigned to them by the system to avoid conflict.

Once inside, the view from the stands was impressive. The arena was about a kilometre and a half below the entrance and had a ceiling about eight hundred metres high in the shape of a flattened cone. The grandstand on which Sam and Tharo took their seats, was yellow, catering to 300,000 spectators or so the information holo stated. Sam saw that there were many other floors hung above them. According to Tharo, this was the largest arena on Zanza, and a total of as many as three million spectators could attend a fight. At each floor, a hologram was generated by eight masts facing each other, giving even the spectators at the top an almost as realistic experience of the battlefield eight hundred metres below as those sitting in the front row.

Sam's eyes were pulled organically to what was the main attraction – the centre of the arena itself where the orange sand was still wet with blood and organic material that dotted the ground.

There was a mixed melee going on in the wide sandy circle, and right then, as screams mingled with jeers and roars of applause, there were people losing their lives.

Every outburst from a fighter below sent a wave of ecstasy through the audience as the fighters used hand-held weapons such as pikes, swords, clubs and lances against each other and against creatures that Sam had no name for. Sam thought of Ghala's wife, who had been swallowed by a Papara in such an arena, and he wondered if he too would see such an eighteen-legged monster today.

There was a final shriek and the pre-show came to an end. The poor unfortunates who had been pitted against fast-moving, bipedal dinosaur-like creatures had all finally been caught. With a chime, the creatures had hissed in distress as their implants controlled their movements and drew them back to the safety cages. The crowd booed even though this was just an initial show and there were far more horrors to be witnessed yet, and the safety cages wheeled back into the opening walls of the area, leaving the ground bloodied and empty.

"Citizens of Zanza!" A deep voice rumbled from a small, fat, colourfully dressed man in the middle of the arena below who had emerged from a hatch under the sand. The crowd, except for two, went wild at hearing his voice. "What a spectacle we have in store for you!"

"Keep moving!" Ehben called gruffly. Behind them, gunshots echoed.

The heavily armed, too-optimistic terrorists, it seemed, were seen long before they even made it to the sewage transport system. Once there, it was up to Oni to tamper with the controls so that at least it would bring them elsewhere other than their starting point until eventually the LPFs managed to override it with them ending up several kilometres below the arena where Sam and Tharo sat. They were deep below the central pillar where the sewage from sixteen main sewers converged and poured into a seemingly bottomless pit.

With all the chaos surrounding them, Ehben had not had the time to check the communicator to discern where exactly this poorly lit pit was leading them. They just had to stay out in front of the troops of the local police force.

They were on a slippery path less than a metre wide on the right side of the filthy network of tunnels. The slightest misstep could cause them to end up in the water and be dragged over the edge.

Not that their demise mattered to any of them in the long run. They were going to die and not one of them doubted it. Ehben now saw in the twilight that the path was dead against the massive base of the pillar with quite a precipice in between.

Arn had just come to the same conclusion. "How deep?" he called to his father.

They stood on a ledge over a deep pit into which emptied pipes of dirty, frothing water. Somewhere down there was the entrance to the reactor, using the water and this shaft as a coolant for its intense mechanical processes.

However, there was the not-so-small fact of sixteen waterfalls that they had to navigate. Or fall through.

Ehben finally forced himself to consult his communicator. Ghala, who had never been able to keep up with them with his short legs, was bound on Arn's shoulders, firing salvo after salvo with a giant cannon to a spot some 150 metres away where the path curved left. Behind Arn ran Oni, the green-feathered Crom, who was clearly reeling from the injuries he had sustained when a shell burst too close. Dark, bluish blood seeped from the feathers at his shoulders and arms, and the bird-creature limped, hissing with pain with every other step. At the very back stood the Olankan with a weapon in each of his five flexible arms. He reacted so quickly that he presented a constant barrage of plasma shots against the officers trying to chase them.

"Ehben!" his estranged son urged him again.

"We are right above the reactor but the water continues for another five thousand metres. Too deep to cross without a vehicle or rope!" Ehben had to struggle to keep his voice heard above the roar of the sixteen waterfalls.

"We have to go down!" shouted Oni now too.

"That's suicide! We could pass the core without realising it!" responded the oldest fiercely. "We could kill the LPFs there and retrace our steps, take a diversion to the reactor."

"We don't have time for that!" Quieter, audible only to his father and Ghala, Arn added, "Then I will go alone."

"You won't." The fire had gone out of Ehben, a defeated father who had recently survived only nine children and would not just stand by and watch his last child also slip from his fingers.

Arn found his fierceness returning. "As a Djockar, I have the fastest reflexes of us all. Therefore, it falls upon me to complete the mission."

Ghala followed the conversation but for once showed enough respect not to interfere in this struggle between a father and his son.

The elderly Djockar took a step forward until he was near his son and said menacingly, "I forbid you to go. Not after all I have had to endure."

"It is my decision and mine alone," Arn spoke as confidently as before. "What was done to my brothers, sisters, my mother and you should never have happened. I will go and make sure the Administrator here does not let anyone else suffer like that ever again."

Ehben hesitated. "Are you sure you want to do this?"

"We are so close. The mission comes first."

Ehben nodded. "Then we will do what we can here to give you as much time as possible."

Ghala jumped off Arn's back.

"Here," Oni said. "You will need this." The Crom handed Arn a tube about twenty centimetres long. He had not been able to follow the conversation but he knew the Djockars' perseverance and their body language had told him enough. Arn would not stop until he had completed the mission, just as his father would not just stop until he had avenged his soon-to-be entire family.

The quiver had a belt at both ends, which Arn used to tie it against his upper body.

Without words, Ehben handed him the communicator.

Until that moment, Inna was still focused on the troops attacking them and had not caught anything of the altercation. Now, like the others, he watched as Arn held the grappling hook firmly in his hands and carefully passed his father to come to a halt at the edge of the precipice. Inna's face twisted in a grimace but they turned back just as quickly to fire another volley down the tunnel. Sacrifice was expected here.

"Five thousand metres," Arn muttered. With his back to his companions, he cast a final glance at the map. "Five thousand metres." He closed his eyes, breathing in and out slowly, trying to shut out the roar of the sewage beneath him. Only when he had sufficiently sharpened his mind did Arn's green eyes open again and Ehben saw his last child facing his demise.

Arn jumped. Before he hit the water, there was a sizzle of blue energy around his head as the in-built field generator in his Survival Respirator (enhanced somewhat by Ghala) activated. It would keep him safe in the toxic waters at least – not that he was going to be safe for long, considering what he was about to do.

"How long before he gets to the core of the reactor, do you think?" asked Ghala after a moment of silence, after watching Arn disappear into the swirling brown water.

For the Crom, it was a simple calculation. "In free fall and with his size? About seven minutes. Slightly longer, since it goes down at an angle."

Ehben let out a low moan at the inevitable loss of his son but there was no time left for mourning as another round of shots from the Zanza LPF's sought them out.

"Hold them back! Give them everything you've got!" Ehben roared, and fired back.

———

The colourfully dressed host looked around the arena with a glower. The listeners hung on his every word.

"It is therefore my honour, friends, my loyal residents, that I present to you, for the twentieth time, this champion, a fighter who continues to test both us and the opponents present him with time and again. Ladies and gentlemen, here he is - the dreaded Metal Butcher of Zanza!"

The crowd went crazy as T750C emerged wearing armour made entirely of chrome, already matte black here and there from numerous burns, scorches, and scrapes.

The metal humanoid, Arti T750C, raised his mechanical arms with a cannon in one, and looked at the millions of spectators who had all flocked to see if he would survive his twentieth encounter.

Sam peered at the Arti. "He still looks pretty fine, no?"

Tharo glanced at his communicator. Almost all the data on his screen was lit with a warning red. "Never rely on what you see. T750C's power source is not without limits. Its battery should have been charged months ago. My gut tells me that it has run on exceedingly low power during its stay here."

"What do we do?"

Tharo shrugged. "There is nothing we can do. This will without a doubt be his last duel."

———

Arn immediately went headfirst and disappeared into the raging waterfalls. He was falling to his death, he knew. But he tried to keep his eyes open because the mission came first.

Water poured all around him, hammering his body as he twisted and plummeted. Somewhere, before the sewage water crashed into whatever bottom, there was the entrance to the subterranean reactor. Arn twisted as he fell. He thought he saw something – a glimmer of incandescent tubing set against the walls...

Arn dove deeper. The beating heart of this megacity had to be nearby. He had to act fast.

Fortunately, the grappling hook had not been knocked out of his hands by the raging water. He had clung to it as if it was a matter of life and death. Which it probably was. He shot...

... and saw the grappling hook ricochet off before falling into the deep.

—

The host pointed to the other corner of the battlefield. "And here comes his new opponent! A creature so terrible that many have lost their lives capturing it. A monster so bloodthirsty that it pierces anyone's heart with fear at the mere sight. Please appreciate this mighty Grog from the Upter System, deep within the Quaat Empire!" The commentator said it with such enthusiasm that the audience joined in. A worthy opponent pointed to an interesting fight.

As the audience applauded wildly and eagerly awaited T750C's opponent, the host sank back down through the hatch in the sand. A pale blue shield shot up and immediately became virtually invisible as the playing field was completely enclosed. The audience went silent, as if someone had turned down a volume knob. On the other side of the battlefield, a leaden gate slowly hissed open.

Events like this could be seen all over Zan and brought in quite a lot of money. Profits that made all this possible and introduced a new fighter to Zanza. T750C was the first one to see him as his opponent: a towering, slime-covered fighter. A creature that, with a single growl, scared the hell out of the spectators before they had even seen him.

Arn felt his arm almost dislocate as the rope tightened. The grappling hook had found hold after all! Fortunately, Arn had also secured it to his belt, otherwise he would have lost his hand from the snatch. The young Djockar, convinced until seconds earlier that he would crash or drown at any moment, or first drown and then crash, swung from one wall to another and smashed into the second wall with a shriek. In the darkness, with the water continuing to pound against his entire body, he lost consciousness.

—

It was common knowledge that behemoths like the Grog, no matter where in Zan they came from, were biologically engineered to withstand Zanza's gravity. Originally, they came from a much lighter gravity planet and, as such, the pre-engineered or 'natural' Grogs could grow far larger and denser than if they had evolved on Zanza or in Terra-normal gravity. The Grogs used for the games had been bred apart from their natural origins however, and their bones were fused with metal to give them more strength and the muscles that were attached to them were big. Together with its skeleton, it was strong enough to not only carry massive unnatural weights but also to manoeuvre without issues. Why? Because the Quaats enjoyed a challenge now and then.

The slimy giant may have been chained but everyone knew that the chains would not hold for long. The beast was so incited by the crowd and the cloud of pheromones that had beforehand been sprayed on Tharo's Arti that he soon sent the first pieces of metal chain flying through the air. The rest was not too long in coming. The furious Grog, finally freed from his chains, roared and made the spectators tremble with fear.

The Grog, comfortable on four legs or two, caught sight of T750C and lowered its giant, shovel-like snout. With a guttural hiss that shook the lower stands, the Grog charged. On different levels, spectators could see on holograms of how the raging ten-tonner stormed towards his opponent. The ground thundered under the enormous weight, and sand was kicked out from under its claws.

This was David against Goliath, thought Sam. As if a Djockar were going up against a Quaat. One small and fast, the other big and strong. The wildly enthusiastic crowd knew this but also knew that a Grog stood no chance against their metal champion who had yet to lose a single match.

T750C had not yet moved. There was no point in shooting at the Grog at random. Only where the skin was thinnest could bullets harm it. The combat Arti raised his guns and carefully aimed his salvos.

Arn's body hung like a rag doll from the wafer-thin rope of the grappling hook several kilometres deep below his companions in the cold darkness. The roar of the waterfalls was in his ears but he hung close to the side of the wall, inside the myriad flows that hammered down the centre of the shaft.

"Ugh...?" Slowly, Arn's eyes flickered as he regained consciousness. The blow against one of the outlet pipes had done him no good. The young Djockar felt at least two broken limbs, a shattered nose, broken teeth and probably a lot of lost blood. He groaned dazedly.

There was no point losing himself in pain and self-pity, he knew. With hypothermic fingers, he reached for the communicator but the thing slipped from his fingers and fell into the raging water. Only one thing remained.

From his pocket, he took out the light source Tharo had thrown into the Nimbas-overgrown shaft. When Arn had picked up the orb, it had immediately stopped emitting light after which he, not without Tharo's knowledge, had wisely stowed it away for later use. He held the object in his fist and pressed it, as he had seen Tharo do. Between his fingers, he saw the sphere glowing and he opened his fist carefully, as he could not lose his only source of light.

About seven metres above his head, he saw the edge. Below him, there was only darkness. Beside him, there was a wall of water. Suddenly, in a flash, he saw the lifeless body of the green-feathered Crom pass into the water and disappear into the depths. A gaping hole on his chest made Arn realise what had happened to the most intelligent member of his team.

Another sacrifice this mission had required. It only gave Arn more energy and perseverance to finish it.

With a simple press of the button on his grappling hook, he was hoisted upwards. The severely injured Djockar reached the dry edge and climbed over it, towards the glimpse of shining crystal tubes he had seen during his plummet.

With a groan and a gasp of pain, Arn dragged himself up onto the small service ledge and with the light of the sphere in his hand, he found himself staring at a network of crystal or glass pipes of all sizes criss-crossing around a concrete pillar. The luminous pipes pulsed and glowed with yellow, white, and blue energies. This ledge was open to the shaft, and it revealed one of the core energy nodes that led to the subterranean reactor itself. Arn understood immediately the reason why it had been placed here. If there was an error in the reactor below, the shaft and the water provided a much needed coolant.

But Arn was going to cause a whole lot more than a mere error, wasn't he?

He did not take time to enjoy the spectacle; he knew he was dying of pain. The Djockar stumbled and crawled on hands and knees over and under the tubes. Somewhere under all this lay the reactor. To go out and find a door or other means of accessing it was, in the state he was in, not going to happen. He would have to take care of that himself.

The furious beast ploughed over the sand of the arena with its long talons. Each attack was slow and predictable but would do a lot of damage to the little Arti if it got hold of it. With every outburst from the Grog, T750C was able to dodge every attack. The mechanical human whirled and spun, jumping backflips and leaping high over each claw sweep with the expertise of a skilled gymnast. It was clearly still the people's champion. As long as the Arti won, as long as his reflexes didn't fail, as long as it could keep attacking the beast at its weak point.

But what the crowd did not notice was what Tharo's observant eyes did see. He had assembled the Arti single-handedly and knew exactly what his metal friend could and could not handle. He seemed to react a fraction slower each time, as if fatigue was starting to play tricks on him. What Tharo had already feared seemed inevitable now. The Metal Butcher of Zanza was about to lose.

But the Arti did not give in easily. At last, its salvos had pierced the thick skin on the beast's neck. Blood, flesh and thick skin were thrown high into the air. The beast roared loudly and moved away from its attacker.

T750C saw the thick tail of the beast coming in his direction but no longer had the energy to get out of the way in time. T750C was hit head-on in the chest and came down on its back with a hard smack over twenty metres away.

At that moment, you could have heard a pin drop in the arena. The metal man was no longer moving. From his chest came white smoke.

The data on Tharo's communicator went from red to a flickering, alarming blood red. T750C's battery showed only 2% energy left.

"He has a few minutes left," Tharo breathed.

T750C lay motionless on the ground, staring at the audience. The connection of Tharo's communicator to the Arti was working both ways, it turned out.

VOICE RECOGNITION ACTIVATED, read the metal man on his visor. SEARCH SUCCESSFUL. THARO LOCATED. The Arti's gaze was drawn to a section of the crowd where on its visor an orange marker lit up. Tharo. Sitting next to him was the Terran of which Tharo had spoken before he departed for this mission.

The Grog stormed forwards. All spectators were on the edge of their seats. They saw that there was still life in the Arti and to stay that way, it would have to start reacting quickly.

From the stands, no one had noticed the green light on T750C's left wrist. The bright spot was in contact with another bright spot: the partially sand-covered weapon it had lost when thrown to the floor. The green light flickered faster and a stable connection was finally established. The weapon slid across the sand towards the Arti at lightning speed and latched onto the metal man's arm. With new ammunition, the fight could still turn around. T750C looked at the beast and launched a new projectile at it. It struck, nestled into the open wound and exploded there. The roaring beast recoiled backwards. Meanwhile, T750C kept firing. Five, six, seven times.

Until the firing abruptly stopped.

The smoke emanating from the Arti's chest suddenly grew thick and dark. Whatever was going on inside the metal body had begun to affect its basic functions. T750C could no longer flex his fingers even to fire the weapon.

—

Arn made a quick prayer for the soul of Oni, who'd had the presence of mind to provide the entire team with a plasma torch. No wall or door was too thick that could withstand the plasma that now came out of the burner at a temperature of 35,000 degrees, with which Arn was now cutting his way through the ceiling of the reactor room. It was thicker than expected but nevertheless the metals still yielded. Finally, Arn had made a full circle and the piece fell away, and he was greeted by a loud splash.

After years of waiting and planning, it was finally there. A brief moment of exultation sang through Arn.

He saw a column of light in the darkness below and clear blue water. In it lay the reactor, Arn knew, although he could not see it. He stuck his head through the round hole and peered inside. Directly below him, he saw pipes connecting the ceiling to the surface of the water. One of them was completely crushed under the massive piece of ceiling he had cut.

"We know you are there, Djockar!"

An angered voice rang out through the dark. It was the voice of someone who clearly did not favour him. "Whatever you are thinking of throwing through that hole, I have a dozen agents here who will neutralise it immediately with..."

Without warning, his troops opened fire on Arn before their commander finished his sentence. The already badly battered Djockar could not dodge whatever they shot at him. Riddled, Arn's body fell through the hole.

The agents saw how the Djockar's broken body land on the thick tube that was damaged by the piece of ceiling and was now sliding into the water. Soon, the body was hidden from their view by a cloud of blood in the reactor coolant.

—

Without the ability to control its fingers, T750C's weapon had become virtually useless. The Arti dropped the gun, straightening up and turning towards the Grog.

The spectators watched tensely and encouraged their champion. It looked like the fight would not last long.

T750C sprang forwards, moving faster than anyone expected as the combat Arti ran towards its opponent.

The beast lashed out. T750C dodged the attack. Two razor-sharp blades as long as forty centimetres slid from the Arti's wrists and with a phenomenal leap, it landed on the monsters tail. The Arti planted the blades into the monster, stabilising himself. The Grog roared out as T750C made its way up, stab by stab. The monster tried but with its short arms, it could not fight off the dark smoke-emitting Arti. The latter went right past the gaping hole in its neck and climbed to the very top, all fifty-three metres high. T750C bent over on one knee on the Grog's head and planted both of its blades as deep as it could into the giant's head.

That's where things went critically wrong.

The black smoke swirling around T750C became a flame, and then guttered out. Lifeless, the Arti sat on top of the Grog's head. Thus ended the fight between David and Goliath. The Grog, although extremely injured and with a high probability of death, had survived the Arti. The crowd of spectators was ecstatic.

WARNING, read T750C's visor.

RESTRICTED DISPLAY ACTIVE.

PRIMARY FUNCTIONS INACTIVE.

SECONDARY FUNCTIONS INACTIVE.

MOVEMENT CAPABILITIES EXHAUSTED.

STATUS CRITICAL.

ENERGY 0.2%.

RESIDUAL EMERGENCY ENERGY 0.001%.

REDIRECT ENERGY TO WRIST IGNITION MECHANISM.

REDIRECTION SUCCESSFUL.

Both blades shot through the Grog's skull, right into his brain. Both opponents had died.

With no grip this time, the Arti fell straight forward and landed between the giant's legs. The Grog itself staggered for a moment and tilted backwards. With a loud thud, the massive body went crashing to the ground. A moment later, the metal man burst apart. A thousand pieces of hot metal flew in all directions.

The spectators couldn't hold it any longer. What a fight!

Tharo bellowed with displeasure, jumping to his feet and beckoning Sam to follow him.

A whole troop of the local police force had gotten up to behind them and had waited for their moment to arrest the two.

THE FREE DEMOCRATIC SYSTEM

Newly published article intended for Page Anonymous

Approximately 780 million U.T.S years ago, an event known as the Volgarian Expansion began. An adventure that lasted for about 670 U.T.S. and eventually led to the beginning of what I sometimes call the Golden Age, or our Utopia. It is a considerable history to catch up on but it is essential to get to the topic I want to write about; the Free Democratic System, or FDS, which we adopted at the beginning of the 55th Age.

But perhaps even more important is to go back to the beginning of the decision-making implants because without this technology, we would not be where we are today. The official start of these implants took place just before this Golden Age after they were inserted into every Zanese. The idea behind it had existed for much, much longer. It was only during this period, somewhere before our Utopia, that they were officially activated and widely used. Fortunately, the implantation procedure was already fully established within the Zanese population and by then was very comfortable, at least according to what I have heard about it.

But why decision-making implants? Because Zan is simply too large and complex for single individuals, or even multiple individuals, to manage and control. The main purpose behind the implants remains unchanged: detailed mapping of the population's needs. What is missing from their lives? What can be improved? Can we take their needs into account in new decisions or modify existing ones to meet those needs?

An important word here is "can" because during the introduction of the implants, all the way until the end of the 54th Age, taking into account the needs of the population was still optional. Yes. Even if the majority of the Zanese people agreed that things should be different, it was still optional. In the 55th Age however, without a governing body, the needs of the people were immediately incorporated into legislation if the majority of the Zanese voted for it.

The idea of letting every person in possession of decision-making implants have their say in deciding Zan's future did not seem like a bad idea at first. However, over time, problems and frustrations began to pile up in Zan, which is evident in the age we live in. Now we face the problem of a Zan becoming increasingly more extreme without a central governing body. In some regions, the situation is so severe that those who have a different opinion are severely punished by their friends, family and acquaintances.

The original idea of a Zan for, by, and of each Zanese had good intentions at the beginning of the 55th Age but it ultimately seems to be turning into a fiasco with unpredictable consequences for the beginning of the 56th Age, if we ever get to that point. We can only wait and see how the situation will evolve and what the future holds.

So why did we allow the people to decide all this if we knew the outcome? Well, because having alternating Ages with a new or recurring model of administration each time can produce both good and bad results. Thanks to the abundance of media, our society has never been more interested in the entirety of Zan, the future of Zan, than we are now. This has even brought the beginning of our Golden Age closer than ever before.

So, in the case of the Ages, the Zanese people clearly know what they want and don't want, and this is constantly being discussed between every Age. In other words, the people are constantly reminded of the past and the lessons learned from it.

It is important to note that switching from one Age into another, unlike the "Welcome to the Family Package" where a new planet is introduced to the rest of Zan and vice versa, does not happen often over the course of several Monster-Years. Similarly, this does not mean that all Ages end in conflict.

Since the start of the Volgarian Expansion, 780 million years U.T.S., which we consider to be the beginning of the 1st Age for the first space-faring species, only 54 Ages have occurred. Some of these Ages were short-lived, while the longest-lived of them was the Utopia itself before it finally came to an end. While I have mentioned that not all Ages end in conflict, I should add that sometimes Zan's star map needs to be thoroughly revised as it has changed significantly. Let us not forget that we once started with 299 territories.

In Zan, we have since seen a colourful collection of rulers; emperors, kings and queens of different species. Sometimes individuals did not even know they were of royal descent, and the Volgarians went to great lengths to track them down. We have had tyrants, presidents and prime ministers, as well as various forms of government, including republics, monarchies, theocracies and dictatorships. All of which was decided upon by the population between Ages. But unfortunately, due to poor leadership or wrong decisions, we have also gone through many conflicts, including seven Great Wars of Zan, in which almost every species and Territory was involved, the damage of which can still be seen today.

Yet, there are two certainties amid all that we have been through: Zan still exists and the current political system is unprecedented. The FDS, as mentioned earlier, is a one of a kind; a Zan that is of, by, and for every Zanese.

CHAPTER 13

Zan: 1983, 55th A.o.Z., a.V.E.

Monster-Méridia Calendar: 1.05.024;

Méridia-Archive Calendar: 2.18;

Terra (UTS): 2628.08.16

Zanza, Zanzia System, Sattar Province, The United
Worlds of Man, Gamma A, Third Circle, Zan

The office inside the pillar to which the two Cattarians were escorted without anyone making a fuss was nothing like the rest of the dingy and dirty city. *Chic*, Sam thought, that was the word. Overly chic, even. The ceiling was lined with gold leaf and under the huge window began a red carpet that covered the entire room. The walls were covered with detailed murals. Sam saw depictions of Zanza's history etched in bronze or made of intersecting tiles. The first probes to descend through the thin atmosphere of a baked and sterile world; the vast Guild machines that created and maintained the atmosphere; the arrival of the first settlers after drone ships had prepared much of the way – and of course, the excavation of the inner planet by giant industrial ships. Vast diamond chandeliers shone above the pitch-black stone desk. From high up in the pillar, the window offered a view over much of the city. Without the smog, it would have been truly spectacular. It was clearly the office of some high-ranking official.

Tharo glanced briefly at the local police forces who lined the doorways that led into the room, and the one they had just entered through. So long as they remained obediently in their places, they did not seem to be looking too intently at them. He muttered to Sam, "Do you still feel the presence of a third party?"

Sam turned to the armed troops and looked at them one by one. All stood idly and emotionless at the various entrances to the room. "Stronger than before even."

"I feel it too. Remember what I told you earlier. Concentrate on the here and now until it becomes acute."

"That won't take long," Sam spoke up. "Even now, whoever it is or whatever it is, is moving towards us." Tharo nodded in agreement.

A door opened and the officers stepped aside to let someone through. A small, fat, colourfully dressed man. It was the host from the arena. The Administrator, Sam guessed.

Behind him walked someone who looked nothing like him. It was a skinny, tall man who, based on what they saw, looked as if he survived on the crumbs of bread the fat man didn't finish.

An Enforcer, Sam and Tharo both knew. Scary people to most but not to them.

Enforcers were wanderers of the law and they did exactly what one might think of. They wandered the stars, travelled within systems, and trekked long distances on both planetary and fabricated surfaces. They entered unsuspecting villages, wandered around communities, and dared enter businesses whether they were open or not. In some cases, when they felt like it, they even dared to enter private properties purely for observation during the day and, if they felt like it, even at night. Wherever they went, they scared the inhabitants and forced them to repent if they had wronged their Lord. The Enforcers searched, listened and executed the law where there was none or where it was in need of correction.

Since the Enforcers were all carefully trained to be more machine than something else, they knew the law so much better than the Guardians for that was their one and only function. If you had nothing to hide, then you had nothing to fear. Their God, they themselves would say, was Zan itself. They truly and fully treated it as a deity, which the Guardians accepted up to a certain degree since it was the people themselves who had voted for their creation.

Usually, a Guardian would intervene only when he walked into an Enforcer doing things to innocent people that, according to the Guardian, went too far. Even then, an Enforcer would find whatever excuse available to him, always referring to the Lord's will to justify his actions. Eventually, the Enforcer would back off, no matter what he said, simply because it knew that a Guardian outranked him. There were stories from the Guardians saying that they had no choice but to kill the Enforcer that opposed them, simply because according to them, the Lord outranks all.

That big man looked at them with disgust and spoke to no one in particular. "Could someone tell me who these dirt-drenched and poorly dressed types are who are soiling my hand-woven carpet?"

The shrill, thin Enforcer whispered something in his ear. In rank, Enforcers, compared to an Administrator, were higher up in the chain and rarely interfered with their job unless their Lord required their interference. This meant that if they hung around, they always interfered anyway.

"Right," the Administrator's eyes narrowed, before taking a seat behind the desk.

"Are you..." began Sam.

"Speak only when Administrator Altar has addressed you," the Enforcer interrupted, after which he referred to both Tharo and Sam using the typical two words Enforcers liked to use on anyone who wronged them.

"Lost ones such as yourselves keep their eyes solely on the ground and do not look your superiors in the eyes. When you answer him, you do so briefly and respectfully and always end those answers using the respectable title that comes with the position, which here is 'Administrator'. Understood?"

"You must forgive my friend here," Administrator Altar interrupted. "Like so many of his kind, he too is without patience and direct, to the point even that this directness might be intimidating. He insisted on joining in meeting you but I think that just this once, we can skip formalities." To which the Enforcer made a slight bow. "So here we all are. We have rarely had to deal with outsiders who manage to break in here. I am Altar, the Administrator of the entire Zanzia system and you, Tharo, have entered my city illegally. Indeed..." Administrator Altar leaned forward with a cocky grin, "I know exactly who you are."

He was bluffing, Tharo knew immediately. The man knew nothing more than his name, which he had given when he arrived at the port.

"Your travelling companion here," the Administrator looked at Sam, "is less notorious. But I will find out about him later. We had noticed you on the surface until we lost you and then we saw you reappearing with us in the Underground."

The Administrator leaned forward. "Don't worry about the rest of your party, by the way. They are currently still pending. It would appear, dear sirs, that you have put yourselves in an awkward position. Why have you come all this way? More importantly, why in the company of a ragtag group of terrorists?" The man seemed irritated by the pair's coolness.

It was Tharo who responded. "Your Butcher of Zanza. That Arti is a member of my crew. He was taken here on the surface after he refused, at the request of your troops, to identify himself, after which those same troops started opening fire on him."

"A member of your crew, you say? Interesting. You are here to reclaim him?" asked Altar mockingly. "Do you then also know that this Arti was not registered anywhere and was only picked up on suspicion of espionage after he not only killed one of my agents but then also tried to extract information from his armour? Are we talking about the same Arti here? Well, you have seen for yourself, there is not much left of your friend."

"That we have seen. That's why I'll settle for just his memory cards."

"Not until we have seen what the Arti's intention was. But now that you are here, you could just tell us."

Both men looked at each other. Sam got the impression that the whole negotiation took place in those few seconds of silence. The Administrator's grin said enough.

Then a door opened. "Well!" spoke the Administrator as Ehben, Ghala and Inna were roughly pushed inside. "Back together at last." He turned to his men. "The others?"

"The Crom died in the sewage and the younger Djockar was shot at the reactor."

"How unfortunate," Altar said slowly, as if he really cared.

Sam saw Ehben's fist tighten, and his eyes flash as he tried to contain his misery. *Poor man!* Sam couldn't comprehend the pain he was going through right now. To lose his entire family in the space of a few days!

"How you managed to bypass the defence systems around the reactor, we have yet to find out. But whatever you were doing there failed."

"Then why did you let us live?" asked Ehben.

Before the Enforcer could also point out to Ehben the applicable rules of manners, the Administrator spoke. "There are too many unanswered questions. Be glad your companions were given a swift death. Yours will not be so merciful."

Altar leaned back and looked at his Human prisoners again. "From now on, your Arti's memory cards belong to the United Worlds of Man," he continued. "There is no point in asking for them, this discussion is closed. Your companion here will be interrogated like the rest and, based on the answers they give us, be subsequently put to death or if it pleases me, released back on the surface of this world. Zanzia will sure enough do the rest. Your life, on the other hand, Tharo, I must spare. Why I do not know but there is someone with an even greater interest than mine, someone who is eager to meet you. The message was to deliver you undamaged."

"I will not settle for that," Tharo replied.

"What you do or do not settle for is of no importance to me. I am the Administrator of this system. I am here because the people appointed me and I answer only to the Guardians of Zan. So do not force me to contact them because what they are capable of doing to spies is far worse. I have the power to do what I want without your opinion being relevant."

And so, Tharo finally knew what he had always thought about the Administrator of the Zanzia System. That he still had not informed the Guardians of Zan with all the fuss reaffirmed that Altar, like so many other Administrators, was just as corrupt. That, among other things, was what his Arti had been doing this whole time. Acquiring information. Looking for evidence of corrupt Administrators and the one or several organisations that had pushed them over the edge. Something, he knew now, was afoot and that the person Tharo had been sensing all along, wanting him unhinged, was most definitely not a Guardian. Now that he focused a bit more, that he was certain.

EXTRACT FROM THE ZAN CHRONICLES

Index: Comic.

Title: The Amazing Adventures of Fenring, Guardian of Zan

[The pair of Guardians, accompanied by both holos of their Ship-Artis, DD2 and DD8 stand bathed in the light coming though the many windows of a floating rescue vessel outside while all around them shadowy machines loom out of the dark. Fenring and Aya, Guardians of Zan, are currently on board the abandoned ghost ship "the Brink" after the Quaat Empire discovered it floating through their Territory.

No one is on board, and there is no sign of them.]

Fenring: Let's start with a trip through the past and gradually return to the present. The disintegrators. What do we know about them?

[Fenring gestures to the shadowy machines around them]

Aya: Well, back in the day, they were revolutionary invention but they've always had problems....

Fenring: Why?

Aya: Because everyone wanted one. Because suddenly there was a machine that was capable of literally pulling apart organic and non-organic material, all the way down to their chemical elements. Building blocks that could then, if you knew how, be used by other machines for a whole range of other things. It was the answer to the waste crisis of the time. Besides, it was also a technology that was for once not created by the Volgarians, which meant it could be recreated.

Fenring: Correct. It was the Guilds who were involved in maintaining Zan, and the Guilds who knew long before that the materials needed to do all that they had to were not without end. It was they who created the very first disintegrators and, after pumping a lot of research and financial resources into them, demanded a fair percentage of minerals or elements from any individual, planets and the like who wanted to use their revolutionary services. There were ships as big, or even bigger, than the Boomer with the sole function of breaking down material that was previously unable to be recycled.

Aya: Of course, much to the dissatisfaction of the general population was that they felt that, like the technology of the Volgarians, it should be made public and free. If there is one word the Guild absolutely hate, then it is exactly that: free. Besides, there was a legitimate fear that once the technology was released, criminals would use it for their own purposes, with even living organisms undoubtedly falling victim. Over time, disintegrators were installed in various stations, colonies, inner- and between stations as well as planets, while also becoming much smaller.

Fenring: Correct. I see that your training is going well. Then suddenly the building plans and all information regarding these machines were on the galactic net. The Guilds refused to give it to the people and so someone hacked the files and released the schematics. Something that was, of course, eagerly exploited on the black market. Millions of disintegrators were made and sold. As a result, anyone who owned a disintegrator without the Guild's permission, according to the Decree of Popylius, would immediately be labelled and treated as a criminal by us Guardians. The official machines were made even smaller and, more importantly, safer, allowing only non-organic materials to be broken down. Besides, the size of the object they had to break down no longer made any difference. But of course, the bigger the object, the bigger the machine. It was also inevitable then that the unofficial machines disappeared over time due to age or a lack of maintenance.

Aya: Until now. Two Ages later, just when tensions between the far-left and right-wing populations have never been higher. Do you really think a few Guardians can prevent all this?

Fenring: No. But we must try for the sake of all Zanese. We Guardians of Zan do not think in terms of left or right, just what matters to Zan. Back to the disintegrators.

[Fenring and Aya walk through the aisles of brooding machinery, each with giant cylinders disappearing backwards into the darkness]

Fenring: Thanks to the research of our Ship-Artis, we can now say with absolute certainty that the missing passengers on the Brink and other ships did decompose. I have informed High Command that the bloodied conditions we found inside the Brink, combined with the intense decomposing smell, were meant to camouflage the use of the disintegrators. Fine particles in the air that could be linked to a disintegrator were found there too.

Aya: So, does it still make sense for us to call in your sources on Isa? Shouldn't we avoid the risk of their discovery?

Fenring: Of course it still makes sense! Now that we know an enemy exists, it is up to us to find them and destroy them. I value my sources but even more the safety of the very people that do not know what's happening. With or against their consent, if they know the answers, they will no doubt give them to us. We'll see what we do once we get there.

[There is a fizz of static through the air as hologram controls light up around Fen and Aya's head]

Boomer: Message to all personnel. We are approaching the outer layer of inhibitors around the Isa Between-Station. We will be leaving LDT-speed in as little as 5 minutes U.T.S. starting now.

Fenring: What is the most valuable element on the black market right now?

Aya: That's hard to say. Fen-Grite is undoubtedly the most expensive there is. As a mineral, 1-gram U.T.S. of the stuff alone is worth just about an entire system.

Fenring: What is the most useful element then?

Aya: The building blocks needed to maintain Zan, which is pretty much 95% of the periodic table. Atmospheric gases like argon, oxygen, nitrogen, carbon dioxide, water vapour and so on for planetary habitability, and for use inside ships and stations. For the ships and stations, just about every kind of metal for construction and maintenance. Without implants, a Human alone for instance consists of more than 90% oxygen, hydrogen, nitrogen, carbon, calcium and phosphorus. You can do a lot with the first three alone, if of course you possess the know-how. Not to mention all the other building blocks that make up a Human. One Human won't give you much. But a hundred or even a thousand of them will.

Fenring: Agreed. The Great Equalisation involved a lot of elements and technology that only the Volgarians know the secret of, which they have never published or revealed its content to anything or anyone. Agreed?

Aya: Agreed.

Fenring: Good. So, there is no one, other than them, who knows how they managed all of that. But unlike the "recipe" used for that purpose, what came next, the chemical composition, from the time they were made public until now, many tens of thousands of generations later are freely available to any Zanese who understands? DD8 and DD2. I want you to compare the chemical compositions of all species created by the Great Equalisation and only the species that disappeared on our 25 ghost ships and then compare them with the chemical compositions of Humans, Thurrock and Quaats. You never know. Look for idiosyncrasies, differences, similarities, and find out what happens when you mix them and so on. After all, there must be a reason why they mainly target just the species from that time. There is something we are undoubtedly missing. Make sure you guys have the results when we come back.

[There is Another fizz of static as the automated voice of the Boomer, the Quaat ship they are attached to, updates them]

Boomer: Attention: the Guardians of Zan are asked to report to the bridge.

[Fenring and Aya walk away from the giant, foreboding machines and eventually walk through an energy wall into the attached Quaat ship. Suddenly, they are surrounded by bright, well-lit, neon rooms. Workers move about their tasks as the Guardians ascend a lift to the bridge of the Boomer. Here they see the large Quaat Captain surrounded by holographic controls. On the largest screen is a picture of a space station shaped like a giant disk seen edge on, with many turrets and domes]

Dropp: The Isa Between-Station, my dear Guardians. Very comical to see how ship after ship, after transmitting our ID-code, seems to be moving away from it as fast as possible. Do I order them to stop or do we keep that for later? We have already received the ID-codes from the ships that bothered to send them, so we can investigate them afterwards if we need to.

Fenring: The LPFs can certainly handle that on their own. But in the meantime, let me use my access credentials to put the station into a security mode and thus shut down just those ships that still intend to flee.

[Sudden orange-red alarms blare out through the Boomer's control bridge]

Boomer: Captain, I am registering a huge energy wave that seems to be coming from within the station!

Dropp: Have they taken it into their heads to attack us?

Boomer: No, Captain. For a moment, there was an anomaly in the gravity in one particular part of the station. Something pulled everything together in no more than a split second, after which a shock wave started to push outwards. The station itself seems to not be affected by it. The ships in the vicinity however, well, that seems to be a different story.

Dropp: Is it coming our way?

Boomer: It is starting to decrease in strength and speed but it will reach us in no more than seventeen U.T.S. seconds, Captain!

Dropp: Shields up!

Emergency message to the crew: A gravitational shock wave is heading our way. Hold on to something. This is going to be a violent one. Contact in 10 seconds, 7, 5, 3, 2...

In Memory of our Fallen Heroes:

The creative team behind the highly popular series of comics
'The Amazing Adventures of…, Guardian of Zan' pays tribute
to the Guardians whose epic adventures brought them wherever
they needed to among the stars. While some characters are
fictional, altered, or kept private for various reasons,
their bravery and dedication to the cause remain real.

We remember those who served, those who gave their all, and those
who live on in our stories. These comics are only made possible
thanks to the immense amount of data that was given to us by the
Guardian High Command, which tells us all we need to know about
the missions and the ultimate sacrifices of our fallen heroes.

In our vast universe, their memories continue to shine
as guiding stars. They remind us of the courage it
takes to protect our way of life and the enduring
spirit of those who never truly fade away.

ABOUT IMPLANTS AND ADMINISTRATORS

Newly published article intended for Page Anonymous

The why of their introduction and what can be done with them is by now well understood. But the 'how', for those worlds not yet familiar with them, is actually quite fascinating. This is because our Free Democracy, our political system without politicians, cannot function without the decision-making implants. Behind the scenes of these implants lurks an army of analysing Artis, or perhaps it is better to say that ALL Artis participate in this. That is right, the Artis, who are responsible for no less than two of the Great Wars in Zan, simultaneously shape and sustain our entire society.

Many of you distrust these Artis, mainly because of the horrors they inflicted during those wars. However, whether you know it or not and whether you like it or not, from the Artis in your body to the Artis in your children's toys and in even ships and stations, they all have the same sub-programme: analysing our society and thus our weaknesses in order to improve them. Information they then relay through channels within the Galactic Net to the Arti High Command inside the Iron Beast which, in turn, works with the Volgarians and ultimately presents new suggestions inside the decision-making implants to improve laws, introduce new legislation, and discard old ones in any system, province, whole territory, and even the entirety of Zan.

This is a very complex system wherein a traveller is constantly informed of sometimes minuscule changes as they enter a system or province. But it is a system that works.

A system where our already understaffed Guardians of Zan are the absolute military institution and maintain order for the benefit of the people and system we are in. It is important to stress that since the beginning of the 55th Age, this institution has never gone against the decisions of the people and since they have no decision-making implants themselves, they always act from a neutral point of view.

So, what is the role of an Administrator in all this? The role is quite large. On paper, Administrators, along with their entourage, are responsible for enforcing the laws in their system. They ensure that the laws are respected and they should normally investigate possible violations and, to the extent of their severity, pass them on to the Guardians. Administrators, unlike the sometimes over the top, almost puritanical Enforcers of the law, are not to be confused with the LPF's. Administrators are elected, regardless of their background, and they can only hold office for a term of no more than a Méridian year, after which the people in that system must appoint a new Administrator with the previous one resuming the life they had before or being elected to perform the same job but in another system.

An honourable job, you would think, but nothing could be further from the truth. Administrators do not have much power or authority. They are elected by the people and have to implement whatever the people decide. If the people are not satisfied, they will make that clear, especially after every Méridian Third when they have to evaluate their Administrator. Never forget that it is not the Guardians who call the shots in Zan, nor the Administrators who sometimes bear the brunt. That honour always lies with the people. However, this does not mean that a Zanese can just do as he pleases. The Administrators have to deal with the frustrations of the people.

It is common knowledge that this is not an easy job. Increasingly, Administrators face a series of threats from disgruntled citizens who, in some cases, turn their words into actions. As a result, Administrators sometimes disappear helplessly and sometimes for good. If they are found at all, it is often not without harm.

To counter these problems and because the Guardians have better things to do, the LPFs, or Local Police Forces, were introduced. Many thousands are employed by the Administrators to provide a degree of authority and security. LPFs report to the Administrators and the Administrators, if necessary, report to the Guardians. As long as they can handle it, they focus mainly on local, stellar crime. However, being an LPF agent is far from an easy job.

But then what about the Enforcers? Well, you could say that they are sort of the wanderers of the law. Meaning that they travel and know Zan legislation better than anyone, to the letter even. They themselves do not get elected. Once an Enforcer, always an Enforcer. But all of that, I promise you, will be part of another one of my stories.

If you are interested in my opinion and you probably are, considering you wouldn't hear or read my drivel otherwise, I note that most LPFs suffer from a great sense of high-mindedness. They are sometimes quick to see themselves as full-fledged Guardians of Zan and behave accordingly when, in reality, their knowledge, experience and training are nowhere near that of the real Guardians. Even the Guardians have to take the reports of Administrators and their LPFs, or what sometimes comes out of their mouths, with a large pinch of salt.

CHAPTER 14

Blood gushed from Arn's gunshot wounds and reddened the water around him. Some of the wounds were undoubtedly life-threatening but if they didn't kill him, then the limited air supply in his lungs would.

With his head back, Arn sank into the water, deeper and deeper. Slowly but surely, he saw the bottom coming closer. There, just a few metres away from his sinking body, he saw the reactor. He had never seen anything so wonderful: a giant nest of glowing coils and cables forming an approximate square. The blue glow this machine produced was hypnotic. Its hum, in a way, was soothing.

One more time, Arn required the utmost of his body and tried swimming towards the reactor.

A bullet rocketed past him. The gunman thought he saw a glimpse of a man but the bloodied water and backlight of the reactor made any visibility difficult.

Arn's vision was flickering in and out of clarity. He could see the glow of the reactor but it was losing definition. He had to push forward towards the glow. He had to make it... Finally, he collided with the soft membrane of the core, which was a translucent veil of material that seemed to cover the entire structure.

In the red blood cloud underwater, out of sight of his attackers, the Djockar reached for the tube on his back and unscrewed the cap. Out came a huge, transparent needle. The tube itself was the bomb.

Without hesitation, Arn plunged the needle straight through the reactor's membrane. Just as Oni had planned, the reactor began sucking the grey goo out of the tube. A few seconds later, the job was done and the tube began to self-destruct by rapidly breaking down. The Artis would spread throughout the entire subterranean network and, after a complex process of changes and a lot of time later, finally blow it into the sky.

It was finally over.

Arn could follow the rest of his party into death. His entire adult life had been in the service of an organisation that called itself the Freedom Fighters of Zanza, and now he had made sure that not only the Administrator but also the United Worlds of Man and all Zanese beyond would never again forget their name.

One last blow remained. Arn looked up and saw the danger symbols on the various power conduits that ran from the reactor all the way to the surface of the water. In those few seconds, he thought back to Tharo and Sam. Or, rather, to the conversation the Djockar had with Tharo when the latter warned him and his party about using such heavy weaponry. With his focus on the tubing above him, the Djockar reached for the weapon on his belt once more for the very last time. He picked out a tube that, looking at the symbols, supplied energy to the storage batteries in and around the city.

He took aim, forcing his vision to sharpen for just a moment before he pulled the trigger. He shot the tube to smithereens. Immediately it exploded and a split-second later, fire raced around the room.

—

Hours before Arn's nanytobom-bomb would rip it to shreds, one of the suburbs exploded with unseen energy. The smog was lit up by a bright light and seconds later, it vomited out a column of fire that rose hundreds of metres above the buildings. A fire so high that it crashed into the rocky dome of the city where it would spread until it finally petered to a stop. On the ground, buildings nearby broke off from their foundations and slammed into their neighbours with overwhelming force.

The long window in the Administrator's office shook and the dull sound reached their ears a split second after. It was immediately followed by another bang, less dull this time. On their right, another explosion had occurred, already several kilometres closer but equally devastating. This time it did not stop at a vibrating window, with cracks already beginning to appear.

For those in the office who were unaware of the terrorists' plans, the spectacle was a nightmare. A disaster of this kind or scale had never taken place in living memory.

To everyone's surprise, Inna took the floor. For the first time, he growled intelligible words. "He... did... it." His voice was heavy, his words slow, and the time between them long.

Tharo caught his gaze in the eyes at the back of Inna's head but wasn't so sure if the explosions were indeed due to the reactor. The explosion that it was meant to make would eradicate them all.

The Enforcer standing behind Altar didn't seem to be able to handle all of what was going on very well. He started breathing heavily. The fear on his countenance was unmistakable. It was as if the crimes committed against his Lord were overwhelming even for him. Utter destruction, Tharo knew, for an Enforcer was only rarely justified. Soon the man was hyperventilating.

Again, another explosion occurred, a little further away from the original neighbourhood that had been hit.

This time it shook the fat, furious Altar out of its staring.

"Don't just stand there gawking!" the Administrator shouted at the armed troops in his service. "Shoot them!"

Even before his words penetrated the minds of the LPFs, the Administrator saw from the corner of his left eye something approaching at a speed so high that his reflexes did not even have time to react.

The tip of the knife that passed through his hand jammed into the surface of the black table. Around the blade of that knife was the Enforcer's hand, who was no longer hyperventilating. He himself started to screech. The Administrator looked at the pierced hand with an equally affected expression and eyes that were wide open. Altar cried out.

The Freedom Fighters took advantage of the confusion. Ehben was the first to disarm his guard. Like a thief in the night, Inna, with swift fingers, reached for the rifle of one of the female LPFs used to keep her prisoner in line. She had not even seen the Olankan coming who had been waiting for this moment. Ghala responded without flinching. The Medotorian lunged at the gun of the cop who had already toppled Ehben. Inna grabbed the woman's neck with two of his free arms and broke it. The roaring Olankan did so with such force that her head swung the other way. Sam had found a rifle of his own and had no intention of abandoning his companions.

In the end, there was only one who didn't seem to care. Tharo, as calm as ever, did not even shy away from his attackers. Apparently, everyone had forgotten that he wasn't able to die.

The skeletal Enforcer beside the Administrator was still looking at the knife in bewilderment. "What?" He seemed unable to say anything else. He did not respond to the shouts of the Administrator, quite the contrary. He cast a glance at Tharo and fell into a swoon. How the man had gotten him to attack the Administrator, he would never understand.

Meanwhile, the troops had recovered from the surprise and fought back. It was the first time, Sam noted, that a well-aimed shot at his body was actually deflected thanks to Tharo and hit the Human who had made the mistake of shooting at him. The outcome of the fight was already decided. The calm that set in for a moment after the last shot seemed like an eternity but in reality, was only short-lived. Soon the back doors of the office flew open and a range of armed agents streamed into the room. Ghala saw immediately that they were hopelessly outnumbered. The Medotorian roared to Tharo for help.

But it was not Tharo who offered them a helping hand. It came from an unexpected source. A deep rumbling, somewhat akin to an overloaded freight train, seemed to be slowly approaching, growing more intense with every metre.

The ground beneath their feet began to tremble. The twenty-metre-wide lookout window shattered. The LPFs hastily sought to hold on but the floor began to split open.

It was the all-consuming force of the cattaran that had pushed out a huge piece of the pillar that supported the entire cave in no time. Everything of stone and metal, and all the unfortunates inside, thundered down in an avalanche of stone. Again, a silence descended, and this time it remained silent. A cloud of dust was all that remained. Visibility up to the edge where until recently the floor had been was virtually nil.

None of the freedom fighters knew what to say. Ghala's mouth hung open in surprise as they watched Sam bring his outstretched arm to the gun again.

"I think I exaggerated somewhat," said the Terran.

"Exaggerated, he says!" cried Ehben to both Humans. "What the hell kind of weird creatures are you people?"

"A pair that just saved your skin," Tharo soothed the Djockar. The latter seemed to calm down.

Given the time constraints, Tharo had no intention of addressing Sam about this any further. Besides, that would only have increased the distrust of the rest of the group.

But he had to at least say something.

"Focus and concentration," he finally told Sam. "Without these two key elements, any use of the cattaran within the flow is nothing more than a waste of energy. Without focus and concentration, deploying the cattaran for destruction only risks your own demise."

"Not to mention ours," Ehben added as Inna and Ghala began gathering weapons. "You may be a bizarre pair but down here, I guess we all are."

"We must hurry," Tharo spoke.

The giant plumes of smoke rising from the toxic smog were wider than the pillar. Another explosion sounded but they could not see it. Far from being the last, they knew. As to why they were so random, they had no idea. They would never find out what caused the explosions.

Out of the corner of his eye, Tharo saw that Ehben, searching for ammunition and any other items that could still come in handy, had picked up a communicator. The man switched on the device and soon found a map of the area.

He turned to the Administrator. "My memory cards?"

The pained man, still stuck to the table under the knife and shivering with the horror at everything he had seen, shook his head. "Never."

"My memory cards, please?" Tharo repeated.

The Administrator didn't budge.

"I don't have time for your time-wasting, Altar. If you don't tell me where they are, I'll rip that hand of yours in two."

"Disassembling and melt-down department," the man muttered immediately. "Six floors below the arena."

"Come on. We need to get out of here before the reactor explodes." Ghala hissed urgently.

"Time to head out," Sam said.

"The lifts!" Ehben said, his eyes shining fiercely with anger and pride. "We can reach the docks in less than five minutes if they are not already sealed off. For the memory cards, we will have to make a stopover."

The Administrator, who had heard the comment about the bomb, was left alone among the corpses of his soldiers and the unconscious body of the Enforcer behind him.

PIECES OF A PUZZLE

Publicly available evidence of the recovered vessel: Tanis.

What is perfection? The answers vary depending on the person answering them. People of faith respond according to whatever religion they follow, normally followed by a boring sermon, right? Those who are not and who are articulate enough then go back to philosophy. In other words, just another stars-damned sermon. The simple-minded Zanese, on the other hand, conveniently dismiss it with the most customary reply, either with an "I don't know" a "fuck off", or a combination of the two. Amarran on the other hand, I obviously couldn't resist asking him, had a different take on it.

"What is perfection? You're standing in it."

You're standing in it? A response I hadn't expected.

It has been a long time since I met another Master, the first of which was Tharo himself! There is no Master older than him, or at least not according to the information we had access to in the Temple. It's quite uncommon for any Cattarian to run into a Master and even rarer to meet more than one. Also, it is rare to see one of them actually using the cattaran. Tharo is quite reserved when it comes to using it. The less, the better, as far as he's concerned. Tharo is one of those "all power corrupts" kind of guy... which is a fine thing to spout when you're the guy with all the power, and are virtually immortal.

"There is no one alive, wiser and more powerful than Tharo. No one. Not even someone like me." Amarran had told me. What a boot-licker.

Judging from what I've seen, I'm still unconvinced by that. I will have to see for myself before I can believe it. The man told me himself, "You're standing in it." And so, when I asked him how it was possible, the answer from his perspective was quite simple.

"In a way that no mortal can obtain. With time and practice, nothing is impossible."

Okay, but that's not what I was asking, smart-arse. Which is what I also told him without beating around the bush too much. I am not interested in the 'how' but more in what is going on inside you, your process of thinking, what is needed to create not just any ship but an entire fleet of impossible ships out of nothing more than scrap metal and not just hold it all together, but actually make it work.

"By starting small."

Another mysterious, useless answer. Frustrating. Maybe it's better not to know. I mean, it wasn't like Amarran wanted to take the time to briefly explain it to me. I might not even understand it even with my many years of experience. But that's not important. And neither is my question, 'what is perfection'? True enough, I am still alive. That, in the end, is what matters. But why? To his question of whether I preferred to choose the alternative, which no doubt had to be certain death, I did not reply.

"The fiasco on Terra was problematic, true, but someone paid a heavy price for it and so that matter for me is closed. You are unpredictable on the one hand, Kotar, and on the other, you possess the cattaran, which makes you valuable. So, if you choose to accede to my request, then you do so in knowing that if you decide to give your unpredictability the upper hand, there is no place in Zan and beyond that where I will not find you." Amarran told me.

But then, what would Amarran actually do to me? The cattaran is rare and valuable, isn't it? Would he really kill me...?

Well, that was how I used to think, and I still don't know the answer.

All I know is that Amarran *did* somehow manage to track me down, despite my best efforts. It turns out the boot-licker had been quite honest about that. What was it Amarran needed me for?

"I want you to find someone I myself cannot."

CHAPTER 15

```
Zan: 1983, 55th A.o.Z., a.V.E.

Monster-Méridia Calendar: 1.05.024;

Méridia-Archive Calendar: 2.18;

Terra (UTS): 2628.08.16

Zanza, Zanzia System, Sattar Province, The United
Worlds of Man, Gamma A, Third Circle, Zan
```

When the elevator door slid aside, everyone with a working olfactory system smelled the iron tang of heavy metals. The reek that hung there took their breath away, so much so that all but Tharo and Ghala knelt down for a moment. The heat was unbearable.

"This is not a healthy environment, we cannot stay here for long," Ehben said to Tharo, the only one, aside from the Medotorian, who didn't appear bothered by it. The latter looked around at the rest of the party and couldn't agree more.

The dozens of Artis working in the smelter paid no attention to them. They were programmed for nothing but dismantling, and that is all they would do until when they themselves would be dismantled by their successors. Everything that was still usable was recycled. Everything else ended up in the smelter after which all of what was put inside would be eventually moulded into new material.

"Tharo," Sam whispered.

The man followed the Terran's gaze.

Half hidden in the smoke stood an Arti, watching them from behind a high desk.

"Block the door and wait here."

Tharo gave two taps on the Medotorian he was carrying on his back, who immediately jumped into the Olankan's hands.

Tharo walked over to the Arti, who addressed him politely. "Welcome to the disassembling and melt-down department. What can this humble Arti help you with?"

"I am looking for the parts of an Arti that was recently brought in. It went by the name T750C. More specifically, I am looking for its five memory cards."

"Five memory cards, you say? VOICE RECOGNITION ACTIVATED!" the metal man suddenly shouted.

Intrigued by this sudden turn of events, Tharo waited for several seconds until the Arti moved again.

"Tharo," it spoke, graciously and respectfully. "To meet you again after all these years, and even here, was the last thing I expected."

The Cattarian was intrigued. "Do we know each other?"

"Not directly. I was one of many under your command in the War of Five Points."

"Five Points ended almost seven Monster-Years ago," Tharo spoke doubtfully. "The fact that you are still functioning now means you undoubtedly have a maintenance card."

"Still as attentive as ever! I am pleased to see you have not changed after all these years. Indeed, when the war was over, I had one installed immediately thanks to a mutual friend of ours, so then I could always improve myself over the centuries. It seemed safer to equip myself with a few more slots for additional memory cards. I had my old cards secured with voice and face recognition, with the necessary self-destruct procedures in case of my own destruction or a hostile takeover, of course."

"You are the one who deactivated the security around the reactor and the city," Tharo realised.

"Breaking into the security system was one of the first things I managed to do since my coming to this place. I also regularly listen in on everything going on within and on the planet. You are lucky that I had noticed you that way already on the surface. After all, the old mine shaft was also secured."

"Then you saved all our lives," Tharo said gratefully, after which he suddenly realised that this Arti had done more than just that. "AnonymousPerson329?"

This Arti, Tharo was sure of it, was the one who had sent him the emergency message in the first place. It looked at Tharo in silence in the few seconds that followed, realising it had fallen through the net. "Apparently it wasn't that anonymous."

"It took a while but who else but the sender of that message would also disable security when they had to in order for us to get all the way to T750C?" Tharo grinned, clearly pleased with solving this small riddle.

"Hmm," the Arti said, "T once told me that I could only contact his emergency contact when he was no longer able to do so. I did what I could to save him from an inevitable demise and unfortunately, I was not capable of more."

It handed Tharo the memory cards, which slid out from a silvered compartment in the Arti's arm. "It was because of your tactical thinking that we were able to win the war a few millennia earlier than expected. You owe me nothing. When I realised exactly who these cards belonged to, I immediately stopped the information transfer. How much was transferred, however, I cannot say."

"Those are worries for later." Tharo put the cards into a capsule that immediately transmitted the information on it to his Ship-Arti, Hanip. "Getting my companions out of here safely is of much greater importance now."

"That's not going to be so easy, I'm afraid. I have been able to give you a safe passage to get here but that is all I can do. The city is burning and it is hermetically sealed to prevent you from leaving. They know it is because of your party. Waiting for you at the docks, there are countless troops to prevent you from escaping."

"Well, there is a solution to every problem," Tharo said calmly, "We'll see about that when we get there."

The Arti said nothing.

"Would you like to come with us?"

"Impossible," it sounded. "From the moment they detect any wrongdoing or if I were to even leave the city, an explosive in my armour will reduce me to scrap metal."

Tharo stilled for a moment, taking this information gravely. Sam, watching and attempting to listen in realised that Tharo had a real respect for the Artis under his care. "If you knew T750C as well as I did, then you know that his arrival here on this planet was not just to make contact with you."

"You refer to the reason for his arrest, no doubt at your behest. He may not have told me what he was looking for but, as I said, I listen to the entire planet and so I have an idea of what it was that T was looking for. The rumours are true. The Administrator here is as corrupt as can be and has agreed to something truly horrific. This planet does not have a lot of time left, and I am not referring to the success of the Freedom Fighters."

"So, what has always been unthinkable is really about to happen. How long does it have left?" Tharo's tone lowered. Sam tried to follow the conversation but he couldn't imagine what was worse than what was already happening to the people here on Zanza.

"Not much longer. Extremists have already started collecting whatever they want to keep, both on the surface as well as below. Soon the disintegrators around Zanza, which have already been installed, inhabitants and all, will take what they can from its upper atmospheric layers as well as from the planet's core until there is nothing left but bare rock. Even then, they will continue taking what they can for as long as it does not affect the entire gravitation inside Zanzia." He paused, then continued.

"After which the extracted resources will eventually disappear on the black market. According to you, how is all this possible without interference from the outside?" Tharo shook his head in horror. An entire planet farmed and reduced to bare materials for corporate gain. This was worse than genocide. It was a xenocide.

"The proposal to break down stations and even entire galaxies, their stars and all the rest to usable raw materials have always been voted down so far, but it is only a matter of time before it becomes legal." The Arti announced, his tone even and emotionless.

"In Zanza's case, it is in fact happening. In fact, you also know that the next vote on such a proposal is not so far away and that every Zanese, wherever they may be and whatever side they are on, will not be particularly happy with whatever the outcome may be. Your concerns are therefore quite justified."

"Are you sure you don't want to join us in that case then?" Tharo asked once more.

"Quite sure. But since the Underground does not have long anyway, I will provide you with cover at the docks. Once there, you will take the ship I've prepared for you that is ready for departure in dock seven."

Tharo said nothing. It was time to go. He thanked the Arti with a simple nod.

"Before you go, Tharo, two more things. Days before your arrival in this system, an individual arrived with a particular interest in that T750C of yours. Someone with a rather exceptional character and who has already caused numerous casualties here. Even more disturbing was the news that many more of him are on the way and may arrive here at any moment. So, know that you may not have much time left."

"That's one thing and the other?"

"A gift from both me and T750C, and believe me when I say that you cannot refuse it. Your Arti is no longer around and so, T and I would like to offer you a new one. An old friend of mine is a not so quite legal Arti dealer on Méridia who has some very rare specimens. I have already uploaded the necessary details of this to your communicator. You decide for yourself what you wish to do with it. Tell him his debt is cleared if he helps you."

"Do you have a name?"

"More than one but when I was employed by you, I was addressed as Eon."

Tharo paused and briefly raised his hand to touch the silvered metal of Eon's own. "Thank you, Eon."

"Nay, thank you, Tharo, for building T750C. I have never met an Arti who cared so much about another Arti. T750C was my friend and I am sorry he is no more."

On that final note, Tharo gestured for the others to follow him as they led their way through the reclamation yard without looking back. Sam felt a shiver of unease. All of the Artis were busy breaking down the detritus of the city for its base minerals but soon they too would be broken.

—

The Underground complex consisted of the entirety of a cave system. If the cave that contained the city and arena was the largest, then that of the docks was certainly the second largest. At a mere 85 kilometres below the city, the cave was the lowest point. Above it, on the very roof of this place, thousands upon thousands of cubic litres of sewage water flowed into a filtration system that would then return it to the city.

Hundreds of hangars stood back-to-back in rows of two in the docks, separated into dozens with bulky or discrete vessels stacked in each. The corridors between the hangars were wide and about thirty metres high. Each hangar was sealed with a force field of glittering blue energy, one in front and one at the top. Between the hangars were dozens of containers stacked in all shapes and sizes. A network of walkways hung over the entire space. The containers were ready to be taken to the right ship by a tangle of cranes.

The peace that usually hung in the docks was soon disrupted when it was overrun by armed troops. An army of vengeful LPFs set up around the towering elevator shafts from which they could occasionally hear the terrible, dull sounds of explosions in the city high above.

In one such shaft, the two Cattarians and a handful of Freedom Fighters swooped down.

"Get ready," the Djockar whispered to his teammates. "Three..."

All but one stood on the tips of their toes.

"Two..."

Sam breathed in deeply and audibly.

"One..."

As quickly as it opened, the door slid shut again. Within his flow, Tharo was aware of everything around him and had closed the door just in time to prevent them from being mowed down by a couple of dozen LPF cops.

Immediately, the elevator shaft exploded, less than a metre above the lift tray in which the Freedom Fighters were sitting.

Outside the shaft, there were a few individuals who immediately had the reflex to take cover. The others did so seconds later, as grit and rocks came tumbling down, knocking into the charging soldiers and flinging them to the floor.

The troops at the other lift shafts had seen the whole event from a distance and were hysterical. In disbelief, they watched the two-hundred-metre-high shaft come down. Tons of stone and metal crashed with a deafening noise onto the walkways, cranes and containers, which in turn also fell and splashed down.

Finally, there was silence. A soft 'ding!' resounded and the door of the lift suddenly opened. The coast was safe or at least safe enough. Tharo stepped outside and Ehben soon followed him.

Ehben looked around him at the damage Tharo had created and shook his head in disbelief. "You Humans and destruction..."

He pointed his rifle at an agent lying among the rubble, begging for help, and finished him off without mercy.

He looked at Sam. "What if you guys ever lose control?"

Sam did not answer. He was aware of a restless feeling and did not want to think about it. He had seen what happened when he lost control. His family had paid dearly for it.

There was something else though, on the edge of his consciousness. The same sensation of being watched but much closer now. Whatever or whoever it was, it was here.

Tharo felt it too. "Ehben, not far from here in dock seven, a ship awaits us. Take the others there before it's too late. Once on board, set course for Sinmrah. That's the nearest Colonial Station; we'll meet there."

"What will you do in the meantime?" asked the old Djockar, somewhat puzzled.

Ghala agreed with him. "This is not the time to split up."

The Olankan, who still carried Ghala on his neck, growled in agreement.

"I'll steal a ship. It's not like there aren't any to choose from."
Tharo flashed a rare grin.

That was not an answer to Ehben's question and they knew it.
Tharo had no intention of wasting time on explanations. He knew
himself that the others would not agree but also that it was pointless
for them to stop him.

"Then I hope you know what you are doing," the elderly Djockar
said with a deep sigh.

He addressed the others. "Come. Tharo will manage. Let's go,
before any more troops arrive."

He walked towards the dock Tharo had pointed out to them, followed by the others.

"I'll see you on the ship," Sam said resignedly, before he too followed the group.

THE UNEXPLAINABLE MYSTERIES OF MAN, PART 2

Newly published article intended for Page Anonymous

My friends and my loyal readers. I am deeply disappointed. Outraged, even, at the manner in which my fellow Humans are treated by certain Zanese people. People who don't know much better and stupidly throw their bigotry towards Mankind online as some kind of trophy they are proud of, and do so with quite a bit of xenophobic language. Adolescents, you would think, but that is far from true. Anyway. None of this is very smart.

I have to ask the question: why?

Well, we are going to try to answer that here today in this second part of the Unexplainable Mysteries of Man. Once we get to the end of this piece, you will know that the hatred for some is pretty deep-rooted in Zanese history and why it might be time to finally put all of this hatred behind us.

Why exactly do I want to talk about it now?

Because I found myself at one of the Between-Stations near the Tar system a while back when I caught an increasingly heated discussion a few tables away between, shall we say, a simpleton of a Djockar and a Droon. Their xenophobic language towards Humans was clearly meant to rile up those present as this kind of discussion can always attract supporters and naysayers.

"There's one over there!" It echoed quickly. Typical and inevitable that I had to experience something like this all over again. As if I myself personally could be held responsible for all of the wrongdoing the entire Human species has ever done in their eyes. If only they knew.

Now, I almost never take part in these kinds of useless discussions, of which it would be much wiser to just walk away from, but since I was the only Human there and do not always appreciate the mistaken opinions of others, I did feel compelled to offer them an answer. But that opportunity was taken away from me by someone who suddenly began to speak up for me. (In all honesty, I can't say I experience this very often.) Soon, the discussion had escalated, tempers heated up, and the argument ended in a brawl. Of course, it did not last long. A Guardian who was already in the area heard the commotion and put an end to it like only a Guardian can, by just walking in the room.

Once safely back onboard the Krom, my thoughts went back to the whole debacle. Why are Humans regarded by so many as, and these are not my words, "the ultimate evil" when surely, they have also done a lot of good? Is it because, compared to all other species, we are the most prevalent in Zan? Humans, you may or may not recall, unlike the other species originated on not one, not two, but indeed three diverse planets: the original Méridia, Rant, and the newly incorporated Terra. Maybe that's why?

Is it jealousy? Jealousy perhaps towards those same Humans from Terra? Not one Terran Human has so far managed to leave the Solaris System. It isn't allowed by law for the time being, and so it won't happen for a long time to come. However, I have heard several reports of Humans, casual residents or passers-by around Solaris, simply being beaten up in nearby systems and stations, sometimes with serious injuries or much worse. It is not for their possessions because, in almost all cases of aggression, the humans own very little of value. They get beaten up simply for what they are. "Humans." Normal Zanese who are unaware of any harm and about whom their aggressors may have been hoping to be from Terra.

Then, why the jealousy? Perhaps it is to do with the reality, now that Ancient Worlds is no longer concerned with that system, that Humans have access to a System containing a treasure trove of minerals that might help a few dozen planets?

The answer is obvious. The original descendants of the United Worlds of Man, the Human race that originally came from Rant, and actually also the Humans of the original Méridia, have been around the longest. They are tough-as-nails go-getters who have managed to adapt to every situation, all in an ever-expanding arena that has been nearly wiped off the map by conflicts with other species several times since their emergence. Conflicts, of which some, in truth were caused by them, one of which ending up in one of the Great Wars. These days however, Humans are unfairly viewed by many as the ultimate evil. Those who really want to understand why they do what they do should really delve into their early galactic history. Yep, they are by essence not always friendly but they have always been pretty pro-Zan as it stands.

Since the beginning of the Human Expansion, the Volgarians have always documented everything thoroughly and made sure that this information can be found within the Zan Chronicles. Indeed, it has all been so long ago that even the Humans, and in doing so basically every other species out there, would have forgotten their own early history were it not for the Volgarians long ago. Humans, and in fact everyone else, have long since ceased to be the fragile, pure species it once was. There is no such thing as a "truly organic species."

That said. Anyone today who actually wants to know what the Humans of the original Méridia and Rant must have looked like, without implants and all that other technology in their bodies, should turn their gaze to the Terrans.

In the final Terran episode of Ancient Worlds, which showed us Terra's inauguration, you could still see how irresponsibly the Humans handled technology and the pollution of their environment. A profligacy that, with her accession, finally came to a stop. Hard work is now being done thanks to the technology that was given to them to reverse the pollution. Had the contact never occurred, had we just let the Humans on Terra do their thing, they would never have gotten through this filter. Filters, for those who don't know, are the natural evolutionary processes through which every civilisation must eventually pass if it is to survive as a species, otherwise it is doomed to extinction.

Pollution is one filter – which brings us to the original Humans of Rant. Every species that experienced the Great Equalisation eventually had to find a way to get through the pollution filter. In other words, they had to not only find a way to solve the pollution that was already there but also find a solution to stop polluting.

In Zan today, there is no such thing as pollution anymore. That is a topic I will definitely talk about in another article.

In short, our products are developed in such a way that they have an extremely long lifespan thanks to the Arompane radiation. Even then, afterwards they can still be recycled. Either by melting them down or transforming them into something else or by throwing them into disintegrators and then using the raw materials to create something new. A simple spoon may have been part of a ship a few hundred thousand Méridian years ago. We can read this deep inside the product where each and every atom is stamped with both a time-location and item stamp. It is therefore difficult for us to imagine how new civilisations like those on Terra used harmful materials that they then simply discarded into nature after sometimes a one-time use. The materials eventually broke down and became part of the habitat and civilisation.

As I said, all of that ultimately brings us back to the question of why the Humans of the original Rant, and all their direct descendants, can sometimes appear so rude. Simple. In their attempts to get through the pollution filter, they have poisoned themselves to such an extent that through all of the Ages, it still has an impact on their actions. As such, it is unavoidable.

So, have they managed to overcome the filter?

Yes and no. Yes, because otherwise they would no longer be around. No, because, to this day, because of what they did to themselves, they still experience difficulties that they have to suppress thanks to the implants that the Volgarians developed especially for them.

In other words, their failings are literally in their blood and are a stage that every species must pass through. However unpleasant Humans can be at times, know, dear reader, and this is very important, that the only true evil in Zan only takes place when someone consciously enters the Forbidden Systems with the intention of causing problems. All else is evolution and all else is overseen by the Volgarians.

Those who judge Mankind within that territory are forgetting two things. First, somewhere in the history of their own species, pre-or post-Great Equalisation, things have happened that they are incapable of imagining. Humanity, and all the other life in all of its forms and from all of its worlds, have experienced change like no other. Second, and more importantly, there have never been any reports of any Humans or other original species pre-Great Equalisation within the Remaining Ten of ever entering the Forbidden Systems once they were introduced. No Human, no Quaat, no-one. Even if they had a good reason for it, they wouldn't dare out for fear of the repercussions from the Guardians of Zan. Remember that the Remaining Ten exist more for symbolic purposes and that they no longer have much power. Yes, they may still have their own military ships but with a limited arsenal of weapons that by law has to be inferior to that of the Guardians. So, you see, some rules are closely followed by even the most obnoxious among us. Regardless of whatever misguided opinions you, dear Reader, has about humanity or any particular species, you must remember this. Humans do not present a threat to anyone. In other words? Relax.

URGENT COMMUNIQUÉ FROM MASTER AMARRAN.

Intended for the Masters of Yesteryear, the Arti
High Command inside the Iron Beast, our Volgarian
allies inside Zan, and those far beyond.

To those for whom I have always held high regards.

Menders. They exist. The Volgarians, having been warned about them via the First Ones, have long since figured that out for themselves.

That they would eventually one day wander in our direction, if they haven't already, has always been a very real possibility. One that we will eventually find out once they are already here or when they get close enough for us to notice them. In that case, in the situation we currently find ourselves in, this interstellar enemy will simply walk all over us.

In response to their existence, the Volgarians have already been doing whatever is possible to stop the possible downfall of Zan. The solution, or one of the solutions over time were, well, us. The Cattarians. The chosen mutants dotted across the Territories who have awakened their inherent genetic power.

When the First Ones left their dire warnings about the Menders, as we know from the Volgarians, they also left us the means to combat them in the form of the biological material from which eventually emerged Grandmaster Tharo. After Tharo came countless others. In any case, the Volgarians had to exercise a considerable amount of patience for this solution as it took millennia to bear fruit!

Over time, as part of the bigger picture and with the Volgarians as moderators, an alliance was created. An organisation that, in the shadows only, worked towards facing the inevitable Mender threat. A coalition known as the Alliance of Three, consisting of the Volgarians who founded it, the Cattarian community, and all of the Artis.

The result of this collaboration was the pursuit and achievement of what is commonly known in the Zan Chronicles as the Golden Age, which we also call the Utopia of Zan. The culmination of what we wanted to achieve in response to the Menders was far out of sight then. What we do know is that it was, to use just one word, *perfection*!

Things were going well, perfectly even, until the moment when the master plan simply crumbled without so much as a word of explanation. Not the Arti High Command and not even the stranded Volgarians inside Zan knew why. To this day, there has been no explanation. This means that we still assume to this day that Messo, from which all of this was orchestrated, that same Messo previously thought to be untraceable and to which only a Volgarian had access to, was wiped out of existence by the same Menders. The result was the disintegration of the utopia that, with the start of the Great Equalisation, has taken several Ages to achieve.

I know that within this Alliance of Three, there is no room for emotions. We simply don't have any but if I did, the emotions I might be feeling now would describe nostalgia, sadness and a longing for better times. Since Messo's probable downfall, this alliance of ours has not come together once. Those who can are trying to do what they believe is still possible but to no avail. There is not much hope left. Anyway. I am sorry it all went the way it did.

Why am I telling you all this? Because it has been quite a few millennia since this alliance communicated with one another. Also, it is because I can now say with absolute certainty that we too, as Cattarians, following the Volgarians, are facing an enemy that may well be our end.

They call themselves Changelings, the Enhanced, and according to the information I have gathered in the meantime from various organisations like the Shoba and the Silver Moon, I have unexpectedly found out that someone has managed to insert the cattaran into beings who previously did not have it. There are beings like us, with our powers, who were never a part of the Volgarian evolutionary plan. Someone has done what we ourselves, after countless of thousands of years of population experiments, have never been able to do.

To my fellow Masters of Yesteryear, I say this: we have done what we could to make it impossible, until now. I can now say with certainty that synthetically created Cattarians exist and that, to them, we are all Demons.

So how, I wonder, should we as a society best respond to such a problem?

CHAPTER 16

Zan: 1983, 55th A.o.Z., a.V.E.

Monster-Méridia Calendar: 1.05.024;

Méridia-Archive Calendar: 2.18;

Terra (UTS): 2628.08.16

Zanza, Zanzia System, Sattar Province, The United
Worlds of Man, Gamma A, Third Circle, Zan

The LPFs made every effort to prevent the four fugitives from reaching dock seven. From a distance, Tharo heard the shots and explosions that assailed his travelling companions without ceasing.

The walls and floor shook, and not only with the firefight going on behind him. Every few minutes there was a deep, groaning thump and a vibration as another part of the city blew up.

What fools you mortals be, Tharo flung the thought back to the LPF officers as they blindly followed their orders, while everything they defended was about to fall around them.

Quietly and in an intense mode of concentration, Tharo moved deeper into the maze of corridors, further away from the docks. The sound of explosions diminished. The walls only trembled, and no longer shook.

The flow told him exactly where to go. In fact, it told him everything. The energy Tharo had access to told him of the clothes his soon to be attacker was wearing.

How many there were, what colour they were, from what material they were made of, and how it was all woven together. Beyond the inside of the clothes, he sensed simple strands of hair. Thousands of them. Some dark, some brown and some slightly lighter. There was skin. Not only skin as a whole but the several layers that formed it. Within the skin, there were nerve endings, travelling through the body, all the way down to the brain. Tharo felt the blood flow within the veins. Organs, muscles, all of it moving. All of it making a sound that only a handful of lifeforms could hear. There were bones, muscles and a whole lot of implants. All of it formed a body. All of it moving, even though the creature was standing or trying to stand perfectly still. A body that was a mere fraction of all the many millions of things he could feel. Many millions more followed, trillions even, as his focus seemed to be ever expanding. A sense that kept providing him with background information. Like a scientific scanner, the flow told him what something was, what materials were used, followed by what these materials were made from and so on. He could feel the dock and beyond, and yes, he could even feel Sam, Ehben, Ghala and Inna the Olankan (the latter of which was clearly not going to survive the ordeal). He could act to help them. He could save Inna but decided against it. He felt that, in this case and no matter the peril, they needed to help themselves. No matter what, Sam would survive today. He had to.

Dock after dock followed, the labyrinth ran endlessly between the stacked containers. Tharo knew he had to go up to the roof of the dock on his right. With a phenomenal leap, he bridged the thirty metres up in one go. Another benefit, of the rebirth was that it had greatly increased his physical performance. Would this impress the man who ached for a confrontation?

The force field under his feet turned white and crunched with every movement.

There he was. Above the docks on the other side, Tharo saw his pursuer. The man in black stood some seventeen metres higher than him on top of the containers. He held a sword and his intentions were quite clear. Hostile. His cattaran, of course, had already told him about his intentions and the sword only underlined them.

At last, thought Tharo.

"So the Changelings have finally thought to reveal themselves?" he bellowed.

The man was not Cattarian. Tharo was certain of it. He knew

every Cattarian by the feel of their energy signature, and Tharo had never met this one. He knew the ones that had died, and he knew about the ones that were missing, and the ones that were still alive.

"I'm not really a fan of swords," Tharo added offhandedly, as his opponent was still yet to make a response.

That was no exaggeration. Tharo had never needed one, let alone practised with one.

But the fact that this man in black possessed the cattaran as well as choosing to wield a sword, was more than interesting. Tharo decided to play along with the game, more out of curiosity than anything else.

The man jumped onto the dock. The game had begun.

—

"Don't stop!" shouted the old Djockar.

It kept on raining impacts. In the containers around them, the bullets left gaping holes with sharp bangs. At the back of the party, a limping Inna had thrown himself into the fray. The Olankan was doing all he could to keep up with Ehben and Sam and protect them against attacks from behind. Ghala was still on his neck. The duo formed a symbiosis and their seven arms attacked the enemy continuously. The pair fired barrage after barrage of shots, and Sam was amazed at how accurate they both were.

"Keep going!" they heard Ehben shouting.

There was a muted roar and the floor shook. Had that been a thrown photon grenade or an aftershock of the collapsing city? Sam didn't know the answer as he careened, caught the wall just in time, and pushed himself onwards, racing to keep pace.

It didn't matter where the danger was coming from. Just that it was coming.

In the front, Ehben and Sam did everything they could to keep the road clear. Between his shots, the Terran used the cattaran to heave two heavy crates, one four metres high and one a paltry forty centi-metres, onto a group of gunmen.

Inna was limping and hissing in pain. Ghala and Inna were finishing off every target they pointed their weapons at but still, the troops behind them only seemed to grow. The Olankan knew that with his injuries, he would not be able to last long. Not far now, they were almost at dock seven.

"Innaaaaaaa!"

When Ehben and Sam heard Ghala roar, they looked back.

The growling creature would never see their life-saving ship ever again. A well-aimed bullet to the head had instantly ended Inna's life.

—

The man in black roared at Tharo with every outburst but to no avail. Tharo was unarmed but possessed a set of rock-solid reflexes. The swordsman became irritated and started chopping at Tharo faster and faster.

Their footwork atop the force field was like a dance of light and the crunching noise became the accompanying music. Tharo approached the edge of the dock. He took a few steps and jumped to the walkway that hung diagonally behind it, anchored some seventy metres high in the ceiling.

Tharo looked down and saw his own blood for the first time in a very long time. Spatters of red dropped and hit the walkway.

The wound was only superficial and the blood may have been limited to just a few drops but the discovery that he could be injured at all took Tharo off guard.

His assailant, who was using the nearby stairs leading up, joined him on the bridge.

"I am your equal," the man announced, in a voice that didn't sound organic at all but electronic. He removed his mask. The man's lower jaw had been heavily impacted and bionically patched. Tharo understood that the vocal cords would therefore be of the same bionic material.

Tharo felt peculiar. He felt tingling, the stimuli of pain. An emotion he had not felt for a thousand years. He rubbed the blood between his fingertips, making an effort to smell and even taste it.

"Amandium," Tharo said somewhat bewildered. "I knew it... A weapon made with amandium. Now if that isn't interesting."

—

The Medotorian had, despite his short legs, never run so fast in his life as he did now. Panting heavily, Ghala dashed into dock seven, the only dock without a force field.

"Ghala!" shouted Ehben as loudly as he could. "Start it up!"

Sam and Ehben looked at each other. They were thinking the same thing: shall we wait for Tharo?

Without the backing of Inna and Ghala, the situation was starting to look grim for them both. The aged Djockar, in particular, had been targeted harshly. A shot went through his ear, shortening a few grey hairs and burned away the skin on the left side of Ehben's head. He went down with a snarl. Sam, not realising in that moment that another well-aimed shot ricocheted off of him and again hit the gunman, realised that the end was in sight for the old man too. The Djockar had lost everything to the Administrator's troops and would soon lose his life.

From out of nowhere, one of the containers exploded, completely obliterating the gunmen attacking them.

Ehben looked at Sam but the latter shook his head. That wasn't me. The bomb?

"Too early..."

A second blast followed, much heavier than the first. A tanker had exploded in one of the docks.

"My compliments," said Tharo. "A weapon made with amandium must have taken you an incredible amount of time and effort to collect and manufacture."

A thick haze of dust had filled the cavern, the result of one of the many explosions occurring throughout the city. The opponents could only sense each other, not see. Tharo's voice carried well across the distance.

"But it must be said," Tharo continued. "To be my equal, you sure know how to produce an enormous amount of dust."

If only his attacker knew that Tharo was not even using one per cent of what he could actually do. Tharo knew very well that could be what his opponent was hoping for. He knew very well not to underestimate him but Tharo was still not impressed.

A huge bang sounded in the distance. Neither man paid any attention to it. Sam was fine, Tharo knew.

"I could sense your cattaran from the moment I sensed your presence." Tharo took a step to the side. The limited visibility did not matter much, as he counted more on the flow than his eyes anyway. This time however, after the cut, even though it was an experiment, he was taking the whole situation a tad more seriously.

A storage container skimmed past him rakishly, thrown into the space where he had been standing a beat ago by the Changeling's power.

"In terms of your mastery of the cattaran, you are clearly not my equal, otherwise you would have known where I was."

Tharo felt a wave from the cattaran building up and targeted the core. A well-aimed attack hurled the man in black out of the cloud of dust he had draped around them just moments before and with a crash, he came to a halt against one of the shipping containers.

He did not see his own sword that came from out of the surrounding dust, impaling him against the metal wall behind him.

The LPF's who had not perished in the vicinity of the explosion perished from the heat it generated. Some were being cooked alive in their armour. Others without protective clothing were clearly being roasted alive. The screams were hellish.

Had the ship been a little closer to dock seven, Sam and Ehben would definitely not have escaped. But even for Ehben, and strangely not for Sam, the heat was unbearable. Ehben began to get rid of all the metal on his body that was beginning to heat up with a raging frenzy. Sam who did not know what was going on just watched.

A third explosion flared up on the other side of the corridor in the middle of the troops attacking them. Above the flames, on a walkway high in the air, stood Eon, the Arti from the disassembling and melt-down department. It was he who helped them, who triggered the explosions.

His projectiles were self-guiding and created a demarcation around the last surviving rebels.

The metal man jumped down into the safe circle he had created and came down smoothly on his mechanical legs, despite jumping from seventy metres high. The Freedom Fighters were surprised by his arrival, and Sam had to restrain Ehben from shooting him.

"It – he's – they're on our side!" Sam shouted into Ehben's ear.

"I promised Tharo that I would provide the necessary cover," said the metal man.

"Every little bit of help is more than welcome," Sam panted gratefully.

"You are still very much alive," the man in black heard Tharo say. His voice seemed to come from far away, although the Cattarian stood less than a metre from him.

The man who was impaled against one of the sides of a container was clearly not there anymore. He drifted in and out of consciousness and must have already lost a lot of blood.

With great difficulty, the Changeling opened his eyes. He saw Tharo looking intently at the hilt protruding from his chest.

"It must have missed your heart by a hair's length. I'm getting old."

In that, Tharo knew, he was not wrong.

The man reached for it.

"Try not to move. The sword is now the only thing keeping your blood from spurting out of your body."

The victim babbled unintelligibly and laughed mockingly, ever louder. "Wherever you go," echoed the bionic vocal cords, "We will find you. Eventually we'll find you all."

"Maybe," Tharo replied without much concern. "But until then, I'll settle for a sample of your blood."

He grabbed the hilt and jerked it free in one motion.

—

Eon began to gradually increase the pressure. Each shot was a hit and followed up the previous one like a barrage of light. The strategic genius jumped from one cover to another.

"We can't wait any longer!" shouted a battered Ehben to Sam, who was fending off the troops with waves of force. He was finding using the cattaran easier and easier now. He could use it to hurl objects but he could also use it like a forcefield, knocking people back.

"He's right," said the Arti.

"Come with us," the Terran called to Eon.

"This is impossible," the Arti repeated his earlier words. "Someone must have your back. Hurry to the ship, now."

"Sam!" Ehben shouted, and grabbed his right arm.

Sam was suddenly pulled to one side as a shot hit the wall near where his head was at. He spun around but Eon was faster, delivering a fatal shot to the wounded LPF who had attempted to assassinate him.

Ehben kept on dragging Sam backwards, towards the door of the ship as Ghala opened it for his travelling companions.

A shadow flung itself through the air, leaping from the same walkway that Eon had jumped earlier. Sam was stumbling through the airlock, looking back to see the stocky form of his black-bearded mentor. In his hand, he held a blood-stained sword.

"Get us the hell out of here!" Ehben yelled to Ghala.

Suddenly they saw Tharo running towards them alongside the metal man.

"There!" said Ghala ecstatically. "Luck remains on our side!"

"Tharo!" said Eon enthusiastically, after which he promptly exploded. The mechanical man had clearly breached the terms of his contract and was being brutally punished for it. After more than 33 millennia, his existence had finally come to an end.

Tharo walked to the open door and stepped in.

Immediately, thanks to the Ship-Arti which Eon had prepared for them, the force field that unlocked the dock lit up again and the platform on which the ship stood started moving.

"Tharo!" The smallest rebel ran to meet the Cattarian with enthusiasm.

The troops outside were bombarding the energetic field around them but they noticed little of that inside. The ship entered a vertical shaft and, with a sudden flare of their thrusters, they disappeared.

Inside the ship, a hologram indicated where in the pitch-black tunnels they were.

"I hope the Ship-Arti will get us to the surface safe and sound," Ehben said wearily, as the ship began to pick up speed. The Djockar had collapsed against one of the flight chairs, blood oozing from his many wounds and gasping for air.

"Whenever you can, set course for the nearest Colonial Station," Tharo said.

Tharo left the trio alone and sought silence. He had a lot to think about. Questions that needed answers, which he had to think about in silence and solitude.

That did not surprise Sam. Within the bond, he would find out exactly what was wrong.

The ship left the Underground through a long, upward tunnel and soon left the Zanzia system behind. The Dévara would make its own way to Tharo and, if it had to, it could blast its way out of port with Hanip, its Ship-Arti at the helm, without too much trouble. It was that or the ship's self-destruction. Hanip would know what to do.

It had been 25 Méridian Thirds, four hundred and twenty-five Terran years, since Ghala had seen the vacuum of space and for Ehben even longer. The reunion with this darkness was a dream they had never even imagined possible.

"No ships in the immediate vicinity," Ghala announced, now seated in one of the control chairs at the helm of the craft, studying the hologram controls, while making minute adjustments to the many buttons and levers.

"Then we've made it," said Ehben.

With the planet in their wake, they transitioned to LDT-speed. They would never return to it. If they had waited any longer, they would still have witnessed the end of the planet's subterranean cities. The triumph of the Freedom Fighters would be observable from space when, finally, the Subterranean of Zanza, a network of metropolises and connecting tunnels, would light up in terrible, fiery, glory.

Arn would have his revenge at last.

EXTRACT FROM THE ZAN CHRONICLES

Index: Comic.

Title: The Amazing Adventures of Fenring, Guardian of Zan

Moofa: Captain Dropp of the Quaat ship of war, Boomer. My name is Moofa. I serve on the Guardian High Command of Zan and, before we begin this meeting, I would like to take a moment to express my gratitude for allowing this to take place aboard your ship and to support both of our Guardians, Fenring and Aya.

Dropp: It is an honour, Councillor Moofa, not only for myself but for the entire crew of the Boomer to welcome you all here. I am very aware of the hierarchy within Zan and thus, the Boomer will do whatever it takes to continue assisting the Guardians until that time they no longer require her services.

Moofa: Once again, our thanks. As protocol demands it, any Captain who responds to a Guardian's request in certain circumstances is therefore a temporary member of this organisation, resulting in your presence at this partial Holo-meeting.

Let us now then proceed to the order of business.

Friends. Colleagues. We are dealing with a situation which is a bizarre incident and potentially dangerous for the rest of Zan. The images you are currently seeing are those of the Isa Between-Station. Inside it, until recently, sat several ten thousand tonnes of matter, spread over hundreds of floors. There were thousands of rooms and untold numbers of lives. What you see is a hollowed-out space, a perfect sphere with a radius of 48 kilometres U.T.S. in which all of that has just dissolved into smoke. That's a tenth of the total mass of the station. Feel free to think about that. I had to do the same. There are weapons, many banned as we all know, that are capable of doing exactly that but not one that can do so without leaving a single trace. So, the one-word question I ask myself is simple. How? Fenring?

Fenring: We were on our way to the Isa Between-Station to speak to the head of a criminal organisation called the Shoba. Jara was a reliable source of mine who might've been able to tell us more about the disintegrators that we now know were definitely being used on the Brink and the other ships Aya investigated earlier.

In fact, the attackers were very specific in who they threw in the machines. We initially thought of a disintegrator when we saw the damage inside Isa but we haven't found any trace of it so far. And since, as is the case with many such stations, the Station-Arti had been tampered with, there is not much to fall back on. What we do have are digital records, specifically the data from all Ship-Artis within the ships in and around the station, as well as from the Artis aboard it.

Everything in the vicinity was very briefly pulled inwards after which everything was suddenly flung to the other side with great violence. The result was a lot of material damage inside the station and casualties outside the eroded section. Curiously, the extreme force of the shock only increased in strength once it had left Isa, as if it was deliberately done to spare the station. This had the result that once it reached the Boomer, even when weakened, it still shook us violently. There was not much material damage, unlike there was to the ships in the vicinity of the station, many of which did not survive.

Moofa: Captain Dropp, does the Boomer have sufficient medical equipment personnel to help those who were injured?

Dropp: More than enough, Councillor, Moofa. The Boomer has fifty medical beds and three times that number of medical Artis and containers full of medical equipment.

Moofa: Aya, you may be the youngest of all Guardians here, but that doesn't mean we don't appreciate your opinion as one. What do you yourself think about this situation?

Aya: I know as little about all this as you, or your fellow councillors. If you want my opinion then you can say that this was either an accident or that it was done on purpose. Either by a weapon we don't know about, or a new kind of disintegrator, which can do what it is made for in seconds and which in addition, like a possible new weapon is undetectable. Or a third option is that someone caused all this.

Moofa: Well, that someone has caused this of that I have no doubt.

Aya: My apologies, councillor, but that's not what I'm talking about. I know how bizarre this will sound in an equally bizarre situation, but what if this was caused by someone who could create such havoc if desired simply by wanting it, and that person either perished in the whole process or walked away from it alive and well?

Moofa: Well, you know how the Guardians operate. No matter how bizarre something sounds, it is a path worth exploring until the case is solved. In other words, you think there are live weapons running around. What do you base that on?

Aya: When the Boomer came out of LDT-speed, there were quite a few ships that, in the few seconds before the Boomer's Ship-Arti detected the shock wave, immediately left the station after receiving our ID-code while some of those around the station immediately jumped into the LDT. Sometime later, when we were busy surveying the damage, despite the quarantine in which we had placed this station, there was still a ship that went into LDT and refused to respond to our messages.

Tartan: Blex.

Fenring: What was it that you said, Councillor Tartan? Blex?

Aya: Blex? As in the Blex of Page Anonymous?

Tartan: One and the same, if indeed Blex consists of only one person.

Dropp: Can anyone enlighten me as to what Page Anonymous is?

Fenring: An online community in which someone can participate in absolute anonymity. Useful for research, social media, and publishing whatever you want. Guardians know and use it because the Black Market does and everything that comes with it. One of the users is Blex, an anonymous blogger who writes mainly about the downfall of our society and how things used to be. As far as we know, Blex is the oldest blogger on Zan because the texts published by Blex have been around for several Ages. That is why there is a suspicion that he or she consists of several people or they are one and the same person, which in turn would indicate that Blex is quite old. But more to the point, his texts are pretty accurate as if he, or again, she or they, were there when they happened. And as far as we know, Blex's arrest is at the top of the Guardian's list. He writes in a lot of detail about the most gruesome circumstances, all of which, since the beginning of his publications until his latest additions, have indeed taken place.

Dropp: And you think this Blex is responsible for this?

Fenring: Some of the things he describes, the way he handles some things, are, well, bizarre and inexplicable. Despite our measures to stop him or his ship in this case, we still haven't managed to stop him. There are Guardians who have spent lifetimes trying to capture whoever is behind Blex, always to no avail. Even now, there is an entire team that will no doubt come here, hoping for something that will lead them to this individual.

Moofa: That team, Fenring, according to new information that has just reached me, appears to already be on its way.

Aya: Are we sure then that it was Blex?

Moofa: As sure as can be, considering whoever is behind it has just published a new message that talks about the disease that is the Shoba from which he liberated Isa from. You were right, Aya... We will proceed as followed.

The team handling Blex will do exactly that. Under no circumstance will any of you interfere with their work. Fenring, keep working with Captain Dropp but be reasonable. If this investigation takes you too far from the Quaat Empire, send the Boomer back home and use another ship. Or, even better, use one of our own better equipped warships.

Aya: Councillor Moofa. I would like to help Fenring further on this.

Moofa: Fenring is more than capable enough to do that on his own, Aya, but I will allow him to keep you informed of his work so that if he asks, you can always consult him should anything else come to mind. You will return to Méridia with the Womack and once you've arrived in Rioo, do whatever you see fit to maintain order.

In Memory of our Fallen Heroes:

The creative team behind the highly popular series of comics
'The Amazing Adventures of…, Guardian of Zan' pays tribute
to the Guardians whose epic adventures brought them wherever
they needed to among the stars. While some characters are
fictional, altered, or kept private for various reasons,
their bravery and dedication to the cause remain real.

We remember those who served, those who gave their all, and those
who live on in our stories. These comics are only made possible
thanks to the immense amount of data that was given to us by the
Guardian High Command, which tells us all we need to know about
the missions and ultimate sacrifices of our fallen heroes.

In our vast universe, their memories continue to shine
as guiding stars. They remind us of the courage it
takes to protect our way of life and the enduring
spirit of those who never truly fade away.

CHAPTER 17

```
Zan: 1983, 55th A.o.Z., a.V.E.

Monster-Méridia Calendar: 1.05.024;

Méridia-Archive Calendar: 2.18;

Terra (UTS): 2628.08.16

Zanza, Zanzia System, Sattar Province, The United
Worlds of Man, Gamma A, Third Circle, Zan
```

He's coming around."

The man heard a voice in the darkness and, somewhere, he was sure that he recognised it. Flashes of his recent fight came back to him. His sword. The dust. The power of the cattaran.

The man who had been left for dead in a pool of his own blood opened his eyes for a moment. All around him were people in the same black robes he himself was wearing.

"Remus," spoke one of the robed forms. "We thought we had lost you."

Weakened, on the verge of death, he stuttered out one word. "... Soren?"

"We were all so worried about you." His supervisor stood over him, looking him straight in the eye. "Do I administer the preppers on him? They could help him recover instantly."

His kin, Loréna, asked it with such a submissiveness that for a moment everyone actually contemplated whether or not Soren would refuse him any possibility of recovery. The underlying tone of concern in her voice had not escaped Soren's notice either.

"Give him just enough to get him out of mortal danger. But woe betide you if they do anything more than that," said one of the forms, in a voice that was firm and laced with scorn.

The long-haired brunette Loréna knew enough. She had been warned.

Soren looked at the severely battered Remus again. "Let him spend the rest of his life scarred, so he will forever be reminded of his hubris in underestimating our opponents. Remus, you have disappointed me. Your mission here was Tharo's memory cards, and the memory cards alone. Instead, you let an attention-seeking Administrator talk you out of it when you should have just grabbed what you needed and left. You believed, somehow, that you could best Tharo. This was pride on your part and pride has no place in our mission."

The man called Soren then sighed. "Look at the damage you've caused." He looked at the man in disappointment.

Remus looked back with hazy eyes. He was still bathed in his own blood and unable to answer.

"What did you achieve? A broken body. You not only lost your weapon but also the blood on it. All too soon. No longer will we be able to operate from within the shadows."

It clearly didn't sit well with Soren. He looked around and saw the devastation Remus had created.

With a sigh, the man turned to speak to the rest of the company in black robes. "You are all my brothers and sisters, not by blood or species, but by the very hell we have all entered and from which we have successfully emerged. This means we go through fire for one another. We all make mistakes at times but reckless behaviour like this cannot be tolerated."

From the corner, four men appeared. Two of them were dragging a certain fat man who was clearly in a lot of pain, and he was thrown at Soren's feet. The fourth one, even though he was found together with the Administrator, seemed to be in perfect health. It was the unhealthy-looking Enforcer. He had his hands at his back and was not in any way bound. In fact, he wasn't even a prisoner.

"Aah... the Administrator!" Soren greeted the small man warmly.

"We found them as they were trying to flee the city," said one of the Changelings.

"Thank you, Bruut. But my friend the Administrator over here seems unable to function normally."

"The Administrator refused to comply," Bruut spoke. "We were therefore forced to break his legs."

"A pity." Soren turned his gaze to the silent Enforcer who, with pitch-black eyes and monk-like robes, stared right back at him. "Was it out of fear of us that you were fleeing, Administrator, or because your world is about to end?"

The fat man was dying of pain and fear of what else they would do to him. He knew well enough what Remus had done out of boredom. The endless screams of the victims would forever be etched into his memory. He enjoyed watching them suffer, and he enjoyed the mutilation. Torturing someone to death through causing the worst pain possible was still one of the few things Remus could derive pleasure from.

That was why the Administrator was unable to utter a single word.

Bruut, however, knew how to find a way around that. He stomped on the man's legs, after which the Administrator started to scream.

"If you choose to remain silent, that is entirely your own choice, Administrator." Soren crouched and watched with a look of compassion.

"Have mercy..." Altar's plea did not have the desired effect, "I thought we had an understanding..."

Soren bent down to the Administrator and said two very simple words. "Not anymore."

"Be pleased, Administrator," Bruut informed the man. "We have done you the kindness that you will not live to see the end of your planet."

Altar was startled and begged for his life. The Administrator even grabbed Soren by the legs but to no avail. There was nothing he could say or do against his inevitable end.

"Stay focused, Administrator. This is important. What has happened here and what lies ahead with this installation is not our concern. That is, or that was, the memory cards of Tharo's Arti. They are gone, that we know, but have they perhaps been duplicated? Where could we find those duplicates?

The Administrator replied.

"This Planetary-Artis mainframe." The man, having accepted his fate, and in an attempt to keep his cool said without a hint of fear in his voice. "Digital information like that is always stored within one of the mainframes of the Planetary-Arti."

Soren raised his hand and immediately a few of his black robed brothers and sisters went to retrieve what the Administrator had told him.

"We meet on the ship," Soren called after his team.

Soren did not even look at the Administrator again. He paid no attention as Bruut tore Altar's life from his body. Instead, Soren was looking at the silent Enforcer.

"My dear Enforcer." Soren addressed him, strangely with a bit more respect than with Altar.

"You were found fleeing the city, knowing full well that we were nearing the planet. So why flee when you could've just as easily awaited our arrival? Don't tell me it's the bomb we keep hearing about. According to what we know, we still have several hours before the inevitable happens."

The Enforcer, with its hands still behind his back, replied. "The fighting that took place here obliterated my ship and so the Administrator, knowing what I could do for him, protecting him from the likes of you, invited me along."

"And why didn't you protect him?"

The skeletal-looking man showed his first true emotional reaction. He gazed at Soren in surprise. "I am an Enforcer, not a Guardian, and thus not some idiot with a death wish. You people are extremely unpredictable, so it is important to decide which battles to fight and which ones to walk away from. Or do you think otherwise?"

"And therein lies the difference. Guardians, serving the people, have nerves of steel and are trained to hold their ground until such bravery is no longer possible. Enforcers have no nerves. They serve their one and only Lord, and they tend to inflict that service on everyone else with preaching and fear."

"That is an inaccurate description, if you ask me." The Enforcer, at that moment, realised once again that they didn't like one another, even though there was an understanding between the two.

"I don't like you." Soren admitted, to which the Enforcer simply grinned.

"You don't need to like me to work with me."

"Work with you?" Soren looked at the rest of his company and saw the grins on the faces of his fellow comrades. "Just to be clear. We are not working together. We've been told to leave the Enforcers be and that is that."

"Of that I am not aware. In fact, I never even heard from you people until I met your Remus over here. It is because of what I've seen that you will also take me with you and introduce me to whoever is in charge."

Soren was utterly surprised and it showed.

"My dear Enforcer. We are but low-level pawns on a board. An iceberg of which me and my team are among many but only at the tip of it. Despite our strengths, we are nothing more than the muscle within a complex and ancient organisation. My comrades report to me. I report to a guy who, in turn, reports to someone higher in charge and from there on up. My chain of command, even to us, is a mystery and of that chain I only know two higher-ups."

"I've seen your Demon, as Remus described him, in action!"

"Really?" This clearly surprised Soren after which he turned to Remus to show him his frustration. The man, covered in blood clearly talked too much. "How did you experience this unholy encounter?"

"If what he told me is true, then he is well out of your league which I hope will be exactly what your friend here will say," the Enforcer shrugged.

"That's disappointing." Soren admitted, looking at Remus. "But strength isn't everything. How about you just tell me what you know instead, after which I'll drop you off at the nearest station or planet within this system so then you can be on your way?"

"There was another one of your Demons with him, an inexperienced one." The Enforcer said slyly, his eyes flickering over Soren before the ascetic man fell silent, as if to send Soren a message saying 'I'm not telling anything else until you take me to your boss.'

The master of the Changelings regarded the Enforcer for a

moment with surprise before abruptly erupting into a bark of laughter.

"You are a stubborn one, aren't you? Fine, I will allow you to come with us but I will not allow you to speak your poison to any of my team members. In fact, you won't say a word. You will be put in stasis until we take you out of it. I advise you now that when we get to where we are going, you will tell us all you know and that when you do, you make it worth our time. My 'boss', as you call him, doesn't deal kindly with time wasters."

FALSE MANIFESTO ADDRESSED TO EACH AND EVERY CITIZEN OF ZAN

My name is Arn. I am the commander of a movement that many generations back started calling itself the Freedom Fighters of Zanza. In the name of this organisation, we Freedom Fighters claim the total destruction of the Underground in what is now known as the Rightful Hammer of Zanza. The network of all 24 metropolises, deep beneath the surface of the planet inside the system of Zanzia, is no more.

I am the eldest son of land and cattle farmer Ehben and Rhynaiia, and I have just learnt that my mother, along with her seven remaining daughters and sons, my brothers and sisters in blood, have been killed in my father's absence by none other than the United Worlds of Man. Why did I do this? Because I cared about not just my planet but the planets of the inhabitants of the worlds that, like Zanza, are being pushed into the same corner.

I had, should my organisation succeed, no intention of leaving any message. I believed that neither I nor my co-conspirators would ever survive, and our actions would speak for us instead.

However, I was wrong. I did survive, as did some of my comrades. After hearing the news of their suffering and to counter the suffering of many others under the yoke of their oppressors, I decided to make a statement anyway and to do so not only in their name but for everyone, every Zanese person. For everyone who sees themselves as a victim, where they lack the courage to act against a system that is far from sustainable.

There is a sickness in Zan, a sickness caused by a severe lack of resources needed to sustain her way of life. Natural celestial bodies, due to the too-high a cost to maintain them, are increasingly being abandoned by those who no longer want to put energy into them. Planets that, because of their location, no longer meet the increasingly stringent criteria are forfeited to richer worlds that, in turn, have the highest chance of survival. This means that there are planets in the habitable zones of their systems given as little maintenance as possible.

All of this is while the stations literally come rolling off the assembly lines day in and day out to meet the ever-increasing stream of refugees who, after many thousands of generations, have no other choice but to leave their world behind and build a new life in a constructed environment. We are supposed to believe that life out there is supposed to be just as comfortable. All of these new Between-Stations, Inner-stations and Colonies being constructed are being done so with the materials and minerals stolen from decommissioned worlds.

The Freedom Fighters of Zanza had no choice but to undertake what will ultimately be a suicide mission. With our actions, we want to send a message to the Remaining Ten and the United Worlds of Man. When you decided to pull the plug so long ago, you didn't just abandon a world but its billions of inhabitants who, as temperatures soared, suffered needlessly. With this message, we want to mobilise every aggrieved individual to do what it takes to save your world. Do not allow the situation like the one we experienced here happen to you. In the coming vote, vote for more extreme policies on the resource crisis or risk a Zanza-like situation. A Zanza that once had lush forests. There were green fields as far as the eye could see and imposing oceans, teeming with life. When the United Worlds of Man withdrew, they not only opened up our doomed world to her star that would slowly cook it but it fell prey to vultures who took whatever resources they could.

So do something and do it while you still can before things really start getting out of hand.

Vote!

Vote not for the abandonment and raping that followed, not of planets like possibly that of your own, but for those of the station that have benefited on our expense.

Only you can stop this madness or decide to be part of it, and thus, succumb to it.

GLOSSARY

Ack, a Between-Station within Djockar Space.

Administrator, an elected official in charge of a star system.

Age (Time Period), a time period within Zan defined by significant changes.

Alliance of Three, an alliance between the Volgarian community, the Arti community, and the Cattarians.

Amandium, a rare metallic substance.

Ancient Worlds, a broadcast reality show live across Zan, featuring uncontacted and 'primitive' worlds.

Arompane Radiation, a sterilisation process that can preserve objects for an almost indefinite, unlimited amount of time.

Arti, commonly used name for all forms of artificial intelligence, including physical embodiments.

Arti High Command, the governing force for all Artis connected to it.

Astrazan, a widely-used drug that can delay ageing.

Azrael Decree, a decree stating that every new system joining the Zan family must undergo quarantine for one full Monster year.

Bactalla, one of the intelligent species within Zan. One of the eight last remaining civilisations of which 299 attended the first ever Zantmoet.

Between-Station, a space station between a star system. Bigger than an inner-station but smaller than the Colonies.

Blind Jump, a ship's leap through space at any speed without a final, predetermined destination.

Bond, a mental connection between two or more individuals, allowing them to communicate or perceive each other's memories despite vast distances.

Boomer, a Quaat ship of war.

Brink, a refugee ship.

Calla, a planet within Sollomon Space.

Cattaran, a type of psychic ability believed to be genetically created that allows the user to manipulate matter using their mind alone.

Cattarian, a being in possession of the Cattaran.

Celestial Body, any natural object in space, such as a star, planet, moon, asteroid, or comet.

Changeling, rumoured to be a criminal organisation or perhaps a cult.

Collector Ship, a ship that collects and processes the dead.

Colonial Station, Station within the Neutral Zone. Bigger than a Between-Station but smaller than Méridia station.

Communicator, a personal communication device used for everyday communication.

Crom, one of the intelligent species within Zan.

Decision-Making Implant, an implant used by each Zanese to assist in making decisions on specific themes or matters.

Decree of Popylius, a law stating that anyone in possession of a disintegrator must first obtain permission from the Waste-Guild.

Demon (Cattarian), a name used by those who fear and know of the Cattarians.

Dévara, an interstellar ship owned by Tharo.

Digital Bell, a digital currency within Zan, used for transactions via the Galactic Net.

Disintegrator, a necessary but also hazardous technology that can break down any physical compound into its constituent parts.

Djockar, one of the intelligent species within Zan and part of the Remaining Ten. One of the eight last remaining civilisations of which 299 attended the first ever Zantmoet.

DNA Confirmation, a process where everything a person touches leaves a trace of their DNA, used to verify their identity. Some devices or systems require DNA confirmation to function.

Droon, one of the intelligent species within Zan.

Dune, a fictional world within a book of the same name, written by Frank Herbert.

Earth, a planet within Volgarian Space.

Elyseve, one of the intelligent species within Zan.

Emotion Blocker, an implant designed for the Guardians of Zan, used to suppress emotions during specific situations.

Enforcer, a lone wanderer of the law, upholding it with unwavering devotion, revering the law itself as a deity.

Enhanced, a Changeling, capable of using what seems to be the cattaran.

Falaka, genetically manipulated crops, cultivated and traded across Zan. Engineered for resilience, yield, and adaptability.

Fen-Grite, the most valuable element on the black market.

Ferorians, a religious organisation known for leading the largest migration out of the known Zan-space that has thereafter vanished without a trace.

First Ones, the mysterious original inhabitants of Zan, a highly diverse society that disappeared long before the Volgarian Expansion.

Flow (Cattaran), a radiant form of energy surrounding a Cattarian, allowing the manipulation of the cattaran.

Forbidden System, a star system of which it is forbidden to enter, typically those inhabited by primitive civilisations within Zan.

Free Democratic System, a form of democracy with no central governing body, where the needs of the people are directly translated into law through decision-making implants and where the elected officials are there purely for symbolic reasons. Introduced at the start of the 55th Age.

Free Space, a territory within Zan.

Freedom Fighters of Zanza, an organisation based on Zanza that fights for a better Zan.

Galactic Long-Distance Race (GLDR), a popular form of competitive sport in Zan.

Galactic Net, a creation of the Volgarians, that allows faster-than light sub-quantum transfer of digital information. Used (amongst many others) for communication, navigation, and entertainment.

Gamma A, one of eight designated sectors within the spatial representation of Zan.

Glider, a vehicle that comes in various shapes and forms.

Golden Age, also known as the Utopia of Zan, long forgotten by many. It was the longest and most prosperous Age in the entirety of Zan's history.

Grandmaster, an administrator of the Temple of the First Ones.

Great Equalisation, a massive uplift across Zan which began in a time when the amount of intelligent life forms was in decline – that gave birth to Zan as a cohesive society.

Great War, an event that can drag each and every territory into the same conflict.

Grog, a creature originating from the Upter system within the Quaat Empire.

Guardian High Command, the governing body responsible for overseeing the Guardians of Zan.

Guardians of Zan, the only official Zan-wide security force, tasked with upholding the laws of the High Council of Zan, and delivering justice.

Guild, a powerful organisation that unites specialists or corporations within a specific trade.

Habitability List, a list in which celestial objects are evaluated for their habitability, ranking how suitable they are for sustaining life and the costs of maintenance required to do so.

Haraka, an area that covers the entire northern hemisphere of the planet Zanza.

Harvest (Quaat), an ancient Quaat custom in which life was cultivated and subsequently harvested to feed their Armours.

Human, one of the intelligent species within Zan and part of the Remaining Ten. One of the eight last remaining civilisations of which 299 attended the first ever Zantmoet.

Hyossas, one of the intelligent species within Zan. One of the eight last remaining civilisations of which 299 attended the first ever Zantmoet.

ID-Code, a unique identifier assigned to every ship and its Captain.

Implant, a small technological device placed in the body, often with specific functions to improve one's overall quality of life.

Inhibitor, a security system deployed around stations, planets, or onboard certain ships. Inhibitors prevent any vessel from entering LDT-speed.

Inner-Station, a space station within a star system. Smaller than the Between-Station.

Interplanetary and -Stellar Association for Sports-related Activities (ISSA), an organisation that oversees and organises space-related sports activities.

Iron Beast (Atmos), an Arti stronghold on the Arti-world of Atmos.

Isa, a Between-Station within the Lubliën Province of Djockar Space.

Kirana, an eight-hooved herbivore.

Krom, an interstellar ship owned by Amarran.

LDT, LDT-Speed, LDT-Engine, or Long-Distance Tunnel, is the technology which enables ships to travel many times faster than the speed of light.

LDT-Highway, a part of an immense network of LDT-routes within Zan.

LPF, or Local Police Force, and the resident planet- colony- or station security force. Often very insular, punitive, and easily corrupted. Vastly inferior to the Guardians of Zan.

Lubliën, a province within Djockar Space.

Mars, a planet within the Solaris system.

Medotorian, one of the intelligent species within Zan.

Memtrast, a megastructure built to encompass an entire star.

Menders, described within a probe as the beings responsible for the destruction of the First Ones, with reports suggesting that they are on their way to Zan.

Méridia (Planet), a planet within the United Worlds of Man and one of the three worlds that saw Human evolution (alongside Terra and Rant).

Méridia (Station), the biggest ever constructed space station and home to many of the administrative and functional bodies of the High Council of Zan.

Méridia-Archive Calendar, the second calendar system used within Zan wherein the Archive orbits Méridia Station in one complete Méridian Year.

Méridian Month, a measurement of time equivalent to one full U.T.S. year.

Méridian Third, a measurement of time equivalent to seventeen U.T.S. years.

Méridian Year, a measurement of time equivalent to 51 U.T.S. years.

Metal Butcher of Zanza, a Zanzian champion known for winning nineteen consecutive fights in the Underground arena.

Minerals (Currency), used within Zan for larger purchases, consisting of materials ranging from liquids to solids, gases, and plasma.

Mining Guild, a powerful trade organisation made up of thousands of mining companies across Zan. It controls resource extraction, sets strict rules, and protects the interests of its members.

Monster Astronomical Unit (MAU), unit of length. Distance between Méridia and Monstrosus: roughly 1,5 light years.

Monster-Méridia Calendar, the third calendar system used within Zan wherein Méridia orbits Monstrosus in one complete Monster Year.

Monstrosus, a black hole in the centre of Zan.

M-Pub, a bar, part of a chain called, M-pubs.

Nanytobom-Bomb, a powerful an illegal bomb made of self-replicating Nano-Artis, designed to multiply rapidly before triggering a massive explosion.

Neutral Zone, a territory within Zan.

Nimbas (Plant), an extremely poisonous plant that thrives only in absolute darkness.

Olankan, one of the intelligent species within Zan.

One Galaxy For All, a movement believing that Zan resides within a walled sphere.

Ordaenian Gator, a beverage from the Ordaenian System.

Ordaenian, a star system within the Neutral Zone.

Osthopat, one of the underground cities within Zanza.

Page Anonymous, a personal platform across digital space that allows users to publish content while maintaining complete anonymity.

Papara, an eighteen-legged creature.

Paradise World, a world considered so beautiful that it is marked as a paradise world.

Planetary Inauguration, an official ceremony where a planet and its system are welcomed into the Zan family.

Planetary Welfare and Preservation Commission (PWPC), the organisation that cares about the welfare and preservation of planets and other celestial objects.

Porok Decree, a decree mandating the creation of a technological wall designed to protect Zanese citizens.

Preppers, a medicine composed of Nano-Artis, designed to cleanse the body of nearly all ailments and, if necessary, aid in recovery from injuries.

Quaat, one of the intelligent species within Zan and part of the Remaining Ten. One of the eight last remaining civilisations of which 299 attended the first ever Zantmoet.

Quaat Armour, living exo-suit of armour that requires near-constant feeding.

Quaat Empire, a territory within Zan.

Ra, a planet within Thurrock Space.

Rant, a planet within the United Worlds of Man. One of the three planets that saw Human evolution (alongside Terra and the original Méridia).

Rebirth, a transformative event that occurs when an individual enters the star within the Temple of the First Ones. Upon emerging, they are no longer mortal but reborn as an immortal, forever changed by the divine energies housed within the ancient structure.

Red Line, a red-coloured sphere, visible only on navigational maps, that marks the outer boundary of the Zan galaxy.

Remaining Ten, the last ten surviving territories on the map of Zan, remnants of a time when there were once 299.

Rioo, a vast area within Méridia.

Satankan, one of the intelligent species within Zan.

Sattar, a province within the United Worlds of Man.

Ship-Arti, an Arti capable of controlling and monitoring everything within a ship.

Shoba, a criminal organisation active across Zan, known for illegal narcotics, racketeering, and smuggling. Notoriously anti-Human.

Sinmrah, a Colonial station within the Neutral Zone.

Solaris, a star system within the Neutral Zone. Before its inauguration known as Forbidden System #703.

Sollomon, one of the intelligent species within Zan and part of the Remaining Ten. One of the eight last remaining civilisations of which 299 attended the first ever Zantmoet.

Sprall, one of the intelligent species within Zan.

Stal-Zanese, someone who abhors technology.

Star Trek, a classic science fiction franchise created by Gene Roddenberry.

Star Wars, a science fantasy franchise created by George Lucas.

Star-Attenuator, a structure capable of regulating the energy output of a star.

Tanis, an interstellar ship owned by Kotar.

Tar, a system within Djockar Space.

Tatooine, a fictional desert planet from the Star Wars universe.

Temple of the First Ones, an ancient structure predating even the Volgarians, discovered by Tharo, and since turned into the training school and home for all Cattarians.

Terra, a planet within the Solaris system and one of the three planets that saw Human evolution (alongside the original Méridia and Rant).

The Amazing Adventures of Fenring, Guardian of Zan, a wildly successful comic series, loosely inspired by the posthumous adventures of certain Guardians. Though fictionalised, it draws from real legends and events, blending myth, satire, and action.

The Black Hole (Application), a former dating app, shut down after leading to numerous victims—mostly Humans—who were misled or manipulated through its use.

The Champions of Zan, a popular form of competitive sport in Zan.

The Great Filter, a powerful event or barrier that has prevented countless underdeveloped worlds from reaching an advanced stage.

The Silver Moon, a criminal organisation that traffics a wide range of sentient species across space.

Third Circle, one of four designated sectors within the spatial representation of Zan.

Thka Decree, a law from the Great Equalisation that made all new technologies public. It led to the creation of many strange and unexpected inventions.

Thurrock, one of the intelligent species within Zan and part of the Remaining Ten. One of the eight last remaining civilisations of which 299 attended the first ever Zantmoet.

Time Shield, a protective field that activates with the ignition of LDT-engines, designed to deceive nature itself into perceiving stillness, masking the craft's incredible speed through the vacuum of space.

Trexlr, a planet within the Quaat Empire.

Underground/Subterranean (Zanza), a network of massive underground cities.

United Territories, a territory within Zan.

United Worlds of Man, a territory within Zan.

Universal Earth/Terra System (U.T.S.), the primary calendar system used within Zan, based on a standard Terran year consisting of 365 days.

Universal Translator, a brain implant given to every resident of Zan, instantly translating spoken language and written text into the user's native tongue or preferred language.

Upter, a system within the Quaat Empire.

Volgarian, one of the intelligent species within Zan and part of the Remaining Ten. One of the eight last remaining civilisations of which 299 attended the first ever Zantmoet.

Volgarian Expansion, an event that marked the beginning of the 1st Age. It chronicles the rise of the Volgarians, the first intelligent race after the First Ones to venture beyond their own system and map the entirety of Zan.

War of Five Points, a historic conflict that brought about great changes within Zan.

Welcome to the Family Package, an initiative marking Zan's full adoption of Terra-based standards, promoting mutual cultural exchange between Zanese and Terrans. It automatically synchronises Zan's calendar, clocks, and measurement units to Terran fixed standards, for a more unified Zan.

Womack, an interstellar ship owned by Aya, a Guardian of Zan.

World-Building Guild, a powerful trade organisation made up of thousands of companies across Zan, specialising in the creation and development of new worlds. It controls terraforming, sets strict regulations, and protects the interests of its members.

Zan, a vast galaxy comprising billions of star systems, countless stations, and a super-diverse society made up of countless species.

Zan Chronicles, a scientifically and historically accurate encyclopaedia covering all aspects of life within Zan. It can be consulted anytime, anywhere, serving as the definitive source of knowledge across the galaxy.

Zanese, a resident of Zan.

Zan Space-Games, an event that occurs once every five Méridian years, lasting twenty weeks of intense competition. Organised by the ISSA (Interplanetary and -Stellar Association for Sports-related Activities).

Zantmoet, rare moments in history when every spacefaring species across Zan came together for a single massive meeting to discuss the future of the galaxy.

Zanza, a planet within the Zanzia system.

Zanzia, a star system within the United Worlds of Man.

Zargan, an area within the northern hemisphere of the planet, Zanza.

Zoptotto III, a planet within Sollomon space.

55th Age of Zan, the current Age in the Zan timeline, also known as the Age of Resources.

AFTERWORD

The age that shaped me (and us)

The biggest and most influential decision I ever made for myself was offered to me in, I think, 1999 in the form of a video cassette tape (remember those?) on which someone who knew my parents had taped a documentary that they then showed me, after which my parents asked me if I was interested. One that involved my early education and health and simply needs to be mentioned. One that, and of this I am convinced, took me on a path that led from A to B, from B to C and so on. You see, at the age of ten, I was not only a wee lad but I was also a big lad with a certain degree of obesity. A lad, - should you be wondering how obese I was -, that had once actually managed to get stuck inside of a wooden maze within a wooden box, maybe 5 X 5 metres on all sides put together by some people at scouts, which they then had to disassemble. It's funny now, looking back, but not so much in the moment.

Therefore, a big shout out to all of the people within and behind the screens of an organisation that, in Dutch, is called Zeepreventorium on the Belgian coast. Let me explain what this institution was. On Wikipedia, a Preventorium in English is described as an institution or building for patients infected with tuberculosis who did not yet have an active form of the disease. Just to be clear, that is not what this was. Zee, translated in English means 'sea', while the preventorium itself was a place where kids simply lived and went to school to work and learn about their health. In other words, it was a rehabilitation centre for children and adolescents struggling with conditions such as asthma, obesity, chronic fatigue syndrome and so on. You can imagine a boarding school but with a strong health component.

As I have said before, I honestly would not be able to tell you what my life would have looked like if I hadn't gone to this place where I would eventually stay for 6 months, and it was me wanting to go there. This particular decision put me on the path to where I am today. I went in overweight and came out having lost nearly 50 kilograms. To put things in perspective: I was 11 at the time, so this was almost half my body weight at the time.

Before I continue with what came after, it should be said that for a pre-teen that I was at the time those 6 months felt more like a full year. I hated being there in the beginning but at the end, I honestly didn't want to leave. This was not a Shawshank Prison-like institute, as we were allowed to go home during the weekends. I will forever be grateful to not only my parents for signing me up but to all those involved. The institute is still going strong and all the people there really affect the lives of children in the best of ways. I went in on the 30th of June, many years ago, and left a changed person exactly six months later.

Again, not a prison.

So, what came after that? The most nostalgic years of my youth, that's for sure! For it was only then that my interest concerning the age that shaped me slowly started picking up speed until it eventually gave way to something entirely different but, at the same time, subject-wise, not really. The result is the second book that you are at this very moment currently holding in your hands or are, hopefully one day, listening to.

Speaking about life changing moments when historical events suddenly touch your personal history. The events in time of which people sometimes ask you those, "where were you when it happened?" questions. It was there that a teacher randomly kicked open the classroom door (overdramatising, I know), going from class to class telling everyone that he has them! The 'them' in this case were the first ever Belgian Euros that I saw, while another was a live broadcast showing the events of 9/11, which happened only a few days before my birthday, making it, indeed, a bit weird.

First of all. Secondary school. This will be short, for I can honestly say that I didn't really enjoy it. I graduated as a baker from a hotel, butchery and baking school in Bruges, a decision that came after having lost all of that weight. I initially wanted to do something in a dietary kitchen as part of the hotel part of that school but unfortunately that was a specialisation year after the original training. Eventually I dropped out of that and switched to baking because as a 13- or 14-year-old I simply did not want to be bothered with having to go to another school. Anyway. I had worked in about 6 bakeries, including a chocolate factory during or shortly after that, and realised quite quickly that a career in baking, pastry, chocolate and so on was not for me.

But it was actually in those years and about the first two years after that that I became really interested in everything that F.A.C.T.S represented. On top of that, I became fascinated with manga, the immense world of the gaming industry and music, and the soundtracks more than anything else of not only film but also of anime, games, and series. I grew up with movies and series like Stars Wars, Highlander, Star Trek, The Mummy, Predator, The Lord of the Rings, Alien, Stargate and Harry Potter. I played games like Pokémon, the Elder Scrolls, Halo, Mass Effect, and Final Fantasy on consoles or handheld devices like the Nintendo 64, Gamecube, the Xbox, and many Gameboys, while reading manga like Dragon Ball, Naruto and so, so many more. All that also resulted in me learning English because I didn't really do that in school.

Now wait a minute!

No books? Actually, no. In fact, I never really got into reading
until I was already some years into my writing. The story of
how I actually realised that maybe I should read some of the
stuff in the genre that I'm writing in is something that, to this
day, I still remember and would like to share with all of you.

Every time I managed to complete a certain round of
something, like finishing the first, second or third rewrite, - in
this case it was the first -, I always ended up in sort of a black
hole where I didn't know what to do. It was then, to sort
of fill that black void, that I started reading self-help books
for writing. These were books on how to create structure,
how to create characters, how to write a good plot, etc.

It was when I sat in my usual coffee place, about half an hour
before closing, that someone, and I distinctively remember this
person being named Caroline whom I had seen before as a regular,
started talking to me and eventually asked me whether or not the
books actually helped me. That's when I realised three things:

That for one, they really didn't help me and that, since realising
that, I never wanted to follow a course or read a book about
writing because I didn't want that to influence my style of writing.

Secondly. I wrote an entire story, a first version of something,
taking place in space, with aliens, technology, territories,
history, etc. without any prep work, with that prep work
being the aliens, technology, territories, history and so
on. After that I gave myself a year to, in a way, create
a shell around the story itself before rewriting it.

Thirdly, and this was the kicker, I asked myself, maybe
I should start reading some stuff in the genre that I was
writing in? That's what I did. I was so excited about this that
I headed over to the nearest second-hand book shop only
to find it closed for the day. The next day, however, I went

back and walked out with the first two series that I would ever read, Douglas Adams' 'The Hitchhiker's Guide to the Galaxy' and the first book in Frank Herberts' Dune series.

That was also how, for a few years, I started my Saturday ritual where I would have breakfast somewhere with a book where, for every page I turned, I would allow myself to take a bite, resulting in me taking sometimes up to three hours to finish my breakfast.

That's how I slowly got myself into reading. These days, however, you could say I'm obsessed and that I'm working hard to catch up reading and listening only in English! At this very moment, I'm reading each and every novel within the Star Wars Legends universe from start to finish, from which I will then continue with the New Canon timeline while listening to Robert Jordan & Brandon Sanderson's The Wheel of Time.

What was I on about before that little sidestep into memory lane? Ah, yes. Remember when in part one I told you that my parents separating was, in a way, a good thing? This is why. My mom, whom I'd like to deeply thank for this, to a certain degree gave me and - even though they will be rolling their eyes when reading this - my siblings an enormous amount of freedom growing up. Freedom to make our own choices and face the consequences of them - like staying up all night at the weekend for some gaming, sometimes not wanting to get out of bed for school the next day, resulting in her leaving for work and me being late and so on. Looking back at that time as an adult, I recognise that as a single mum, trying to earn enough money and take care of us, she simply did not have the energy to also closely manage her little gang of teenagers - we, the youngest three brothers are close in age - but it is a testament to her parenting skills that we never ended up doing extremely stupid things.

Speaking of my siblings, they too definitely deserve a certain amount of praise for making me, me. I therefore have to thank my

three brothers and, especially my oldest one. Despite him being
8 years older or maybe because of that, I have always felt that I
as a teenager, I have shared with him the best of times growing
up. All four of us shared the same interest – gaming – and had a
good amount of humour. Back then, my oldest brother already
had a place of his own and it was there that myself and my two
other brothers regularly used to hang out at the weekends, from
Friday after school all the way through to Sunday with sometimes
barely any sleep. There was a lot of fast-food in those days and a
severe lack of sleep sometimes but also a lot of laughter and fun.

Thank you!

I also include my sister and her family in here who have
traded in the unreliable Belgian weather for a vastly
better climate of Tasmania, Australia. Know that I
care about and miss all of you in my own way.

Why am I mentioning all of this? Because it not only takes me
back to times that I'm really nostalgic about but also because
it was in those days that my inspiration and imagination really
started to take shape. Even though I started to create that which
later became the Welcome & Goodbye, Earth series when I was
about nineteen years old, I had actually already attempted to write
something on several occasions earlier but it had never stuck.
The reason for this, I think, was that I actually never was able to
write with focus needed for writing a series within the house I
grew up in and was living in at the time. Writing outside however,
somewhere else, really helped me, so that's exactly what I did in
the first few years when writing became a hobby that got out of
hand until I eventually moved out of the house. To know more
about that, you will be able to read what you are looking for at
the end of volume number three, which in my opinion will be the
most fun to write because it's the most recent that I can remember.

Benjamin Wuyts

PREVIEW – THE VOLGARIAN PROMISE

LUNACY

I'm alive! I'm alive! I'm alive! I'm alive!

Okay, but how?

How can you mess up an assignment so badly and still make it out alive after an audience with the obviously disgruntled Master Amarran? How?

Well, by accepting an assignment that I know can only end one way. In disaster. In other words, this is nothing more than a suicide mission. If I fail, I die by the hand of Master Amarran. If I manage it, then I die by either the hand, a simple virus, or by a stupid accident or short circuit , whether it's caused intentionally or not by the Arti High Command. Wherever I would go, even far beyond the Red Line, they will find me and settle the score thereafter.

Either way, it looks like I am ankle deep in the shit.

Why can't Amarran do all that himself? Because A, this is a suicide mission and Amarran wouldn't take the risk and B, the Artis would track him down and he doesn't want to risk us scaring off this particular Arti.

"But you yourself cannot die, Master Amarran. With your ability, wouldn't it be easier to get this assignment done yourself?"

Apparently not.

The Master has a reputation to uphold and while he might not be killed if he were in my shoes, he would still probably fail – and we can't have that, can we?

"But in any case, won't that reputation be tainted anyway if the Arti High Command captures me and gets me to talk?"

And you know what Amarran said then? "We'll see about that once it comes to it but I trust in your ability."

Does the Master not realise that I might be the last person he should entrust such a thing to? Does he not realise that I don't exactly excel mentally in this kind of situation? That I have – according to his own reports – a history of volatility?

Wait a minute. Do I have mental problems or not? Maybe he is testing me with this assignment. Maybe he knows something that I myself have not yet realised.

Wait. Wait. Ambassador Xantos's route, there and back, in the many thousands of years he has been taking them, has been known by none other than the Arti High Command. Taking him into custody on Atmos or Méridia is lunacy.

"Indeed. And apart from the fact that your Ship-Arti is one that is not linked to the Arti Collective, I have nothing more I can say than can help you." The Master had added.

Lunacy. Great. Send a lunatic on a lunatic mission. This is just going to work out swell, isn't it?

CHANGELINGS, PART 1

Newly published article intended for Page Anonymous

There are those who claim that my way of working can be gruesome, while many others among you are of the opinion that it cannot be gruesome enough. If you find yourself taking an unhealthy pleasure in my reports, I recommend seeking help. Whatever you as a reader may think about it, the truth is that I do not enjoy what I do but how I extract information gets results.

But Mister Blex, what if the victim is indeed innocent – I hear you ask? First and foremost, not a single one of my victims is innocent, let that be clear. Anyone who is a member of a criminal organisation or has knowledge of such an organisation and does absolutely nothing about it is definitely guilty. Secondly, I myself do not place much faith in the prison system. I apply my own way of atoning myself to those who are entitled to it. Third, I request everyone to not delude yourselves. Even our Guardians of Zan sometimes have to operate with a heavy hand to get the information they seek. Their excuse is that they consider themselves entitled to do so.

Why am I mentioning all this? Because I want to make it clear that the stories about me and what I am capable of doing are not exaggerated. I want to make you realise that the fear that some of you feel when reading all of these negative messages about my person is not un-warranted.

Not only do the Guardians of Zan read my page here on Page Anony-mous in an attempt to track me down but you who are my kin as well, a readership of many thousands of brothers and sisters. But, according to my sources, there is another group who is paying attention. They call themselves Changelings or the Enhanced, which is what this new series will be about. In the interests of journalism, I will start sharing a bit more about myself to you guys and especially to them.

There are quite a few rumours going around, so allow me to clarify for you. This Page Anonymous account you are reading right now by way of screen, holo, device or direct neural transfer is about a 533,000 U.T.S. years old. In U.T.S. terms, you can read two new publications every week, sometimes on new topics, but since it is hard to find new topics these days as everything has already been discussed, they are mostly existing topics that I re-discuss in a new fresh way. Two publications per week, 52 Terran weeks in one Terran year, multiplied by 533,000 years. Do the math yourself... or don't.

Why am I mentioning this? Because a lot is going on right now and a lot is about to change. But that's not the only reason, though. In fact, the Changelings have triggered something very personal in me.

Who the fuck are the Changelings? Zanese who have managed to achieve the impossible.

They are, I would say, a new breed of like-minded people. A new breed of Zanese who, to get what they want, hunt down individuals like myself. With all this in mind, I want to make it clear to them for a moment that they won't succeed in any way and that they don't quite realise what they have awakened.

Since the first publication of Blex on Page Anonymous up until now and the countless others that will certainly follow, this account has been maintained by one and the same person. Myself, a being at least as old as 533,000 years. Up to you to doubt this or not.

Know this, dear reader, whoever and wherever you are. If you already think that what I sometimes do to my victims is horrific, then you haven't seen anything yet. The Changelings, I know, get quite a bit of help from certain other organisations. So be aware that among you, the Changelings and the readers who help them, there will be no place where you can feel safe and that a quick death in your case will not always be guaranteed.

To the Changelings themselves, I say this: you have managed to stay under the radar for a long time but no longer. This is where it ends. The Cattarians know of your existence and it will be us Cattarians who will do whatever is needed to stop you by any means necessary.

The hunt for the Changelings is on. I, Blex, am guaranteed to confront you in due time. But know that if I don't, then surely someone else will, and that you should expect no mercy.

So, welcome all to this new adventure we shall be calling 'the Changelings.'

Thank you for reading The Unsustainable Systems. If you enjoyed it, then consider leaving behind a review on either Goodreads or Amazon.

For more information on upcoming books, please visit www.benjaminwuyts.com, or consider signing up for my newsletter.

Benjamin Wuyts